The car spun a~~~~~~~~~~~~ pass.

Browne dropped into a crouch, double-actioned three fast rounds, and smiled as the gunner in the backseat catapulted backwards.

Lee jumped directly into the path of the vehicle. He squeezed the M-16's trigger and held it tightly in a full-automatic death burst. The rounds plowed into the front of the car and the windshield vanished into indistinguishable pieces. The driver was riveted against the back of his seat as the death missiles bolted him to the upholstery and perforated his upper torso.

Carl Browne and Marc Lee saw it coming.

The car headed into the undercarriage of an Amoco gasoline tanker. The impact sheared the top from the vehicle. A valve severed from the bottom of the tanker and created a gaping hole flooded with gasoline. The volatile substance only needed one spark.

There was a flash, and the car, tanker, and gunners became an intense orange fireball.

In a microinstant, the tanker erupted like a volcano.

OVERLOAD, Book 1

PERSONAL WAR

Bob Ham

BANTAM BOOKS
NEW YORK · TORONTO · LONDON · SYDNEY · AUCKLAND

PERSONAL WAR
A Bantam Book / June 1989

ISBN 0-553-27709-X

Published simultaneously in the United States and Canada

———————————————————————
•

Bantam Books are published by Bantam Books, a division of Bantam Doubleday
Dell Publishing Group, Inc. Its trademark, consisting of the words "Bantam
Books" and the portrayal of a rooster, is Registered in U.S. Patent and
Trademark Office and in other countries. Marca Registrada. Bantam Books, 666
Fifth Avenue, New York, New York 10103.

———————————————————————
PRINTED IN THE UNITED STATES OF AMERICA

O   0 9 8 7 6 5 4 3 2 1

For my Daddy and Mother, who have always remained an island of refuge unselfishly abundant with love, support, and caring—

and

For Terry, Leslie, and Rob, who have, somehow, managed to endure our own personal wars—

With all my love.

It is well that war is so horrible, else we should grow fond of it.

—GENERAL ROBERT E. LEE
at the Battle of Fredericksburg,
1862

———

Perhaps the most effective way to assure eternal freedom, lasting peace, and true justice, is to intensify the latent threat of forceful retribution.

—MARC LEE

CHAPTER ONE

His eyes focused on cold, tempered steel. It was in their hands and in their eyes. It was at that moment J. T. Boswell fully realized the two men were deadly serious. The peaceful silence of the morning and the soft easy-listening music from the radio on his desk had been shattered by the sounds of his office door flying open from the massive impact of a kick. His visitors were not only unannounced, they were unexpected and unwelcome. He thought the anonymous telephone calls of previous days had been from pranksters. Some sick dysfunctional playing an even sicker joke. His mind wouldn't permit him to believe the mob really wanted to take over his business. After all, Boswell Trucking was his life and New York was off somewhere in another world, over fifteen hundred miles away.

J. T. Boswell had built his thriving Texas enterprise with the sweat of his brow and the brawn of his aging back. By big-business standards, his trucking company was insignificant. He was a mere fish in an ocean of corporate whales. But for J. T. Boswell, his independent trucking company provided a comfortable livelihood. A way to survive. The only way he knew. He'd die before he'd let some wise guys take over the fruits of his lifelong labor.

The lights still burned brightly in Boswell's quiet, plain office located off the loading dock, although it was 12:59 A.M. according to the clock on his desk radio. His gray steel desk was cluttered with week-old paperwork. Behind him, gray metal bookcases held volumes of tariff, routing, and rating manuals. Two straight-backed chairs, seldom used by guests, collected dust in one corner of the room.

1

He could hear outside, into the Dallas darkness over the sounds of the soft music. The night was strangely still, almost chilling. He heard an alley cat's mating call from somewhere inside the company compound. Through the windows he could see the security lights, lighting the turnaround near the loading docks. Beyond the two intruders, through the open door, he could see the lot where local delivery trucks sat filled with freight for deliveries in Dallas–Fort Worth just after sunrise.

It was not unusual for Boswell to be working past midnight. His small, yet busy operation demanded his full attention and the paperwork seemed endless. For thirty-five years he had spared no effort to insure the success of his enterprises. But now . . . this.

The two men, dressed in business suits, had yet to say a word. They just stood there inside the door, clutching their weapons, staring at Boswell.

The music stopped and the one o'clock news came on the radio, breaking the deathly silence. One of the intruders closed the office door, shutting out the outside world.

Boswell detected a refracted ray of light off the edge of a short samurai sword in the right hand of the taller man. The sword appeared to be no more than eighteen inches long. In true samurai fashion, it was surgically sharp. Lethal. He had seen this kind of weapon behead a man with one clean flash through the air. That had been during the Big War, in the hands of skilled Japanese warriors. But what, he wondered, was an Anglo mafioso henchman doing with such a weapon?

The second man, although shorter and less muscular, appeared no less deadly. The twin steel barrels of the sawed-off shotgun athwart his right hip were awesome. From where Boswell stood, they appeared as massive twin sections of corrugated pipe, the kind he hauled quite frequently with four of his Dorsey flatbed rigs. The thought flashed through his mind that he had never seen a twelve-gauge look so damn big. It had been extensively modified. In place of the usual shoulder stock was a rough pistol grip. The barrels terminated at the end of the walnut forend.

Overall, he calculated the weapon to be no more than fourteen inches. He further surmised the little gun would sever him at the abdomen if the stone-faced goon's finger twitched on the trigger.

Boswell stood motionless beside his desk. He felt diamonds of perspiration collecting on his balding scalp. He could sense from his own labored breathing that his face was beginning to turn pale, and he felt light-headed.

He remembered the old Colt Government Model .45 in his desk drawer. He hadn't fired it in years and this was certainly no time for a function test. But at least it gave him an option. He reasoned it might be worth a try if he couldn't talk his way out of this one.

Finally the words came: "What is this? You can't come bashing your way in here like that. Who the hell do you think you are?" It was all he could think to say.

"Shut up, fatso." The taller man with the samurai blade spoke cold and hard. "We're here on business. You've been warned. We're here to make the final buyout offer. And I mean final. Your little gold mine here is of strategic importance to certain people with whom we are associated. In other words, lardass, you're in the way. You should have sold when you had the chance."

"I don't understand what you're talking about." He was bluffing, but he knew it wasn't working. "Whatever it is you want, just take it. Anything. Just take it and leave."

"I like it when they beg, don't you, Bruno?" It was the smaller man with the twelve-gauge speaking now, his acne-scarred face split with a sadistic smile. "Think I should just shoot his balls off and let him bleed to death?"

"Not yet, we need to transact some business first," the bigger man said.

"You want money? Please, there's a checkbook here in my desk drawer. I don't keep cash. I'll write your employers a check." He motioned toward the desk drawer with his right hand.

"Touch that desk and you'll be picking your intestines off of it, lardass. I'll slice your gut open like a ripe tomato."

Bruno set his jaw, gritted his teeth, and with his right hand lifted the sword into a striking position.

It was then J. T. Boswell smelled it.

Death.

"Hey, Bruno, why don't we let the lardass write us a check? What say?" As he spoke, the shorter man never changed the aim of his sawed-off shotgun. "What do you think, Bruno, ten g's?"

"Sure, ten thousand," Bruno said.

"I'll need the checkbook," Boswell said. "It's still in the drawer."

"Okay," Bruno said. "Get it, but don't try to be cute."

"Right, nothing heroic." Boswell opened the desk drawer and felt for the checkbook. He found it, took it from the drawer, and opened it to the next check in sequence. "How shall I make it?"

"Just make the check to cash," Bruno answered sharply.

"Right, cash." Boswell knew he had to make a move, but when? How would he know when?

He wrote the check and tore it from the brown three-ring checkbook. He handed it to the man nearest him. The short one.

Boswell closed the checkbook and returned it to the drawer. His hand raked over the hidden Colt.

He knew it was time—now or never. And he was afraid.

In one smooth motion, Boswell gripped the old Colt .45, cleared the drawer, and tried to fire. Before he could cock and discharge the auto pistol, the man with the samurai sword struck. A gleaming streak of polished steel moved at lightning speed. The sharp surgical edge of the instrument met with flesh and bone between Boswell's right elbow and hand. The hand and the auto pistol dropped to the floor amid a shower of blood and severed bone.

For a microinstant, Boswell felt faint. There was no pain. Then he saw the flash of the mighty twelve-gauge as both barrels spat hellfire. What was left of J. T. Boswell's body crumpled to the floor.

Boswell Trucking could now be acquired by the organization, and Bruno and his associate were ten thousand dollars richer.

There was only one more sales call to make before the two businessmen could head for the Bahamas for a few days of R and R. Later in the morning they would open negotiations with the final holdout, the owner of Leeco Freight Lines. The two men knew he, too, could be convinced.

———

Dale Upton figured he had about ten more minutes before the forklifts finished loading in the forty-eight-foot Fruehauf trailer. The veteran driver relaxed in the driver's lounge, waiting for the dock foreman to call him. He sipped a Pepsi and casually watched the afternoon segment of the national news. Suddenly his attention focused fully on the television. A TV reporter held his microphone into the face of a black-clad warrior.

The soldier was Major Marc Lee, field commander of the U.S. Army's Delta Force. Lee had successfully led Delta Force troops into Libya and rescued forty-three American hostages held at the airport in Tripoli.

Dale Upton listened intently.

"Major Lee, can you tell us any official estimates of terrorist casualties?"

"I have no official estimate. Any further comment will have to come from Delta Force Command or the secretary of the army," Lee responded crisply.

"Major, you and the men of Delta Force are being called American heroes. How does that affect you?"

"My men and I were simply doing the job we were trained for."

"Will Delta Force strike against terrorism again?"

"You'll have to ask the president of the United States. He's the boss."

"Thank you, Major Lee. I'm sure I speak for the former hostages and the American people when I say thank you and Delta Force for a magnificent rescue." The reporter faced the camera. "This is Charles Michaels reporting from the French island of Corsica."

"Son of a bitch," Upton said under his breath. "That's the boss's kid."

"Dale!" the dock foreman yelled. "You're loaded and ready to roll."

"Be right out."

Dale Upton signed the consignment sheets and entered the load into his travel log. He walked around the giant cab-over White Road Commander Two and checked the tractor. He visually checked the tires and hydraulic hoses on the Fruehauf. He closed the swinging double doors on the back of the trailer and secured the safety latch. He inserted a metal seal with embossed numbers on it through the door handle and fastened the ends together. The doors couldn't be opened without breaking the seal. The numbers embossed into the thin metal strip were recorded on the cargo's shipping manifest. The undisturbed seal would satisfy the ICC and insurance companies in the unlikely event the load turned up short or missing. Upton inserted a Master padlock through the lock loop on the door handle and secured the door on thirty million small arms ammunition primers destined for a midwestern sporting goods jobber.

Upton climbed aboard the cab of the big White and fired the diesel engine. The Cummins power plant whined, then caught. He let it idle for a few moments as he mentally traced the route he would take to the Buckeye State. Satisfied the engine had reached temperature, he shifted into first and pulled away from the loading dock. He drove through the yard and out of the gates of the huge manufacturing facility. He read the sign above the gate as he left the yard: OMARK-CCI-SPEER . . . HOME OF THE GOOD OLE BOYS.

Dale Upton left the banks of the Snake River and headed for U.S. Highway 12 East, which would take him from the plant in Lewiston, Idaho, for his Midwest run. He had decided to run U.S. 12 to Lolo, Montana, swing north on U.S. 93 to Missoula, and catch Interstate 90 East. He always enjoyed the trip to Lewiston. It was big timber country, the home of one of the world's largest lumber mills. Upton thought the view along U.S. 12, also known as the Lewis and Clark Highway, was always magnificent. He liked the ride through the Nez Percé Indian Reservation. He occasionally stopped along the way to pick up an Indian novelty to take home to his children.

Dale Upton had decided years ago that driving a truck was the only way of life for him. Sometimes it was fun. Sometimes it was tiring. But even at its worst, driving was always interesting. Runs like the "CCI run," as it was called, were fun. The sheer beauty of the heavily forested mountains, frequently capped with snow, brought America to life before him. He felt a sense of peace and tranquility on the open road.

Dale Upton also liked his White Road Commander. He had equipped the cab-over sleeper with all the comforts of home, right down to a microwave oven to heat coffee or sausage biscuits. The big red machine glittered in the sun's rays as dark diesel smoke chugged from its twin chrome exhaust stacks. The silver Fruehauf cargo trailer proudly displayed large red and blue letters on each side: LFL, the logo for Leeco Freight Lines. Beneath the logo, small letters indicated Dallas, Texas, as the home base of the operation. Old man Lee liked to advertise.

Upton switched his Cobra CB radio to channel 19 and listened to other truckers giving Smokey reports. Bears were sparse and traffic eastbound was moderate to nonexistent. The last reported police car was sixty miles away. Dale Upton put the hammer down and settled back in his airshock seat. He placed a Reba McEntire cassette tape into his Pioneer tape player and cranked up the volume.

The big Road Commander pulled the load through the high country as Dale Upton shifted through the gears. He was making good time, running at least sixty-five miles per hour.

Dale Upton sang along with the lyrics he knew so well.

A massive cyclonic explosion rocked the earth.

The White Road Commander Two, the Fruehauf trailer, thirty million small arms primers, and Dale Upton disintegrated into fiery fragments that shot skyward in an incredible blast that dug a 290-foot crater into U.S. 12.

CHAPTER TWO

Captain Carl Browne threw the last of his overnight bags into the blue-over-dark-blue Dodge Ram Charger 4 × 4. He looked up at Marc Lee with a smile. "Man, I sure do need this break. Thirty days ain't much, baby, but it sure beats spendin' Christmas on a military base."

"I'm glad you decided to come with me. You'll enjoy Texas. It's a hell of a lot better than Libya." Marc Lee looked squarely at Carl Browne. The two men had decided to take their thirty days of R and R in Texas with Lee's family. It was Christmas and they were both ready for a break.

Lee's Dodge Ram was fully equipped with military communications equipment. Delta Command in Washington kept twenty-four-hour tabs on the two men. It was mandatory to be able to contact them at a moment's notice. Terrorists didn't observe American holidays. An FM-VHF high-band transceiver linked them into a nationwide network of digitally scrambled radio repeaters that duplexed into ComSat-D, a strategic military satellite elliptically orbiting twenty-five thousand miles above the East Coast of the United States. By selecting the proper backbone frequency on the mobile rig or one of the portable transceivers they always had available, they could access CSD, the military acronym for the ultra-top-secret Continuous Strategic Defense, from anywhere in the United States. They were never supposed to be out of contact with Delta Command. General A. J. Rogers II at the Joint Chiefs could contact them by simply keying into the nationwide backbone communications system. Each man also carried a

Motorola digital pager which could be activated by the satellite-repeater system. They were never away from the watchful eye of ComSat-D and General Rogers as long as they carried the pager or the handheld.

The unique CSD military communications system had been Lee's brainchild, his own high-tech design. It had also been one of the reasons for his fast progress through the ranks since joining the Army. His passions were weapons and communications, no doubt about it. The man was not only *a* certified communications and weapons expert, he was *the* certified expert for the U.S. Army, CSD, and ComSat-D.

Carl Browne had met Marc Lee when they joined the Army in 1976. They went through basic together at Fort Campbell in southern Kentucky. For Browne, it hadn't been that far from home. He was born in Memphis, Tennessee, but orphaned at the age of nine. His grandmother had raised him in Nashville. He grew up in North Nashville, just off of Interstate 40 at Eighth Avenue. He attended Pearl-Cohn High School and graduated a football and basketball star. He thought about college, entertained some scholarship offers, but when his grandmother died he decided to join the service instead.

Marc Lee and Carl Browne grew close during basic training. Both men scored high on Officer Candidate School exams. Once basic was finished, they immediately entered Officer Candidate School. They graduated second lieutenants. The camaraderie of basic and OCS endured and the two men were drawn closer together by their mutual fondness for weapons and strategy. They had also developed mutual respect for each other's physical and mental abilities as their training intensified.

Lee and Browne tested for Special Forces and both were selected. Specialized training followed, and soon the men were an inseparable team—each an outstanding candidate with outstanding individual specialties.

The bonds and the mutual respect grew stronger when both men were selected for Delta Force. They were stationed together at Fort Campbell, Fort Dix, and Fort

Bragg. When military action came in the Falklands, El Salvador, Grenada, and Honduras, Lee and Browne were there as a team.

Carl was more naturally athletic than Marc. He was a Fifth Degree Black Belt in Korean Tae Kwon Do. He was also a weapons expert and a specialist at field interrogations and counterterrorism. He knew how to deal with men who placed no value on human life. He knew how to make a captive spill his guts . . . one way or the other.

The fall weather was cool but pleasant as the two men traveled beneath a cloudless December sky. It would be a long ride from Fort Bragg, North Carolina, to Dallas, Texas. Once they got to Interstate 40 in Asheville, it would be smooth sailing. They estimated twenty-four hours on the road. An army Learjet was always at their disposal, but they preferred to drive and see the countryside. It gave them time to relax and reflect.

Marc Lee and Carl Browne knew each other inside out; they were comfortable—they were a team.

The plan called for a short stop in Nashville to visit Carl's grandmother's grave, then Interstate 40 into Little Rock and on to Dallas for a quiet Texas-style Christmas.

———

"Mr. Lee, what is it?" Jill Lanier, the petite blond secretary, looked up from her desk and saw the big Texan standing in the doorway to his office. He was pale and shaken.

"Dale Upton," the elder Marcus Lee replied faintly. "The load on the CCI run. It exploded yesterday. That last phone call was from the Idaho Highway Patrol. The only thing they found big enough to identify was the bottom piece of the Idaho fuel sticker from the side of the cab. Dale never knew what hit him."

"Oh, my God!" Jill burst into tears and ran to the ladies' room.

Marcus Lee just stood there in the outer office. He couldn't believe it. Dale Upton . . . gone.

Suddenly the big Texas businessman looked his age. He felt more than sixty at that moment. He couldn't figure it. What had happened? The lines on his face became exaggerated against the shadow of his sandy gray hair.

He looked around the room. Looking, but not seeing. Thick-cut pile carpeting on the floors. Solid walnut desks. Rows of walnut-framed bookcases and filing cabinet enclosures. A small mainframe IBM computer system to make his routing life easier. He had it all and his offices reflected that. They had more the appearance of law offices than a trucking company headquarters. Business had been good. Dale Upton's tragedy was his first major accident in thirty-five years of business. And to make matters worse, there was the Upton family. It was Christmas, for God's sake. What would he tell the man's children?

He hadn't noticed the men walk into his office.

He broke his vacant stare from the floor and looked up to see the faces of two men. "Yes, gentlemen, what can I do for you?" he asked.

"The question isn't what you can do for *us*, it's what *we* can do for you. We can save your business, Mr. Lee," the taller man replied, his voice cold and sharp. His accent was that of a street punk from New York City.

"I'm afraid I don't understand."

"Just say we're in the insurance business. We're here to insure your continued good health and livelihood."

"What is this? What are you talking about?" Lee responded angrily.

"Accidents. Like trucks and cargo evaporating into the Idaho sky. Does that mean anything to you?"

"You mean—you—you bastards—" Lee lunged at the intruders, but a solid left hook caught him on the cheekbone. The big Texan lost his balance from the impact of the huge fist and tumbled to the floor. He shook his head, regained his composure, and tried to stand. Suddenly he was looking squarely into the twin barrels of a twelve-gauge sawed-off shotgun. The smaller man aimed it directly at his face. The larger man held a short samurai sword in his right hand.

"Let just say we all know what a couple of pounds of well-placed C-4 can do to a truckload of highly explosive primers. It's amazing. Wish I'd been there to see that one. I'll bet it was a big, big bang. Anyway, we're here to make you an offer. All you have to do is sign over controlling interest in your business and go away for a nice long vacation. Our people will come in and run the day-to-day operation. You'll get enough income to live comfortably. But more importantly, you'll get to live."

"You're crazy. If you think I'll ever give up control of this company, you're out of your New York minds. I built this company with my bare hands. I built it. I run it. And I sign the checks. No damned way." Lee's voice was filled with blazing anger in an attempt to disguise the fear and confusion he felt. He tried to ignore the ugly weapons held by the intruders.

"You have a poor attitude on business negotiations, Mr. Lee." The big street goon reached under his coat. He brought out a package wrapped in plain brown paper. He gripped the paper by a corner and flipped it. The elongated roll of paper unraveled quickly as its contents fell free of the wrapping. The contents dropped to the floor at Marcus Lee's feet.

Lee suddenly thought he was going to throw up.

The man with the blade laughed. "That's the hand your fellow Dallas businessman J. T. Boswell used to sign his checks. He didn't know how to take care of business, either. Now he doesn't need his hand anymore."

"My God, you're sick. Get out of here. Now!" Lee shouted this time, trying to keep the sour fluids of his stomach from rising into his mouth.

"Right, we're leaving. We'll even give you some time to consider our offer. We'll be back at eight o'clock Friday night to accept your signature on the necessary legal documents. If you don't want to give that to us, we'll take your life instead. How's that for a business proposition, Mr. Lee? Have a nice day."

The two men backed to the office door and left quickly. Lee tried to regain his composure. He sat down in the secretary's chair and cupped his face in his hands—they were cold and moist. He felt his stomach churn and chill bumps dotted his skin. He knew one more look at J. T. Boswell's hand and he would vomit all over everything.

Jill Lanier stepped from the ladies' room. She was now as pale as her boss, tears of grief and shock lining her cheeks. "Mr. Lee, what was that all about? Who were those people?"

Marcus Lee looked up from his hands and faced Jill. "It was nothing, Jill. Just some New York street punks trying to shove their weight around. Forget about it. It never happened. Right now, I've got to go tell Dale Upton's family. God, I don't know how to do it."

Then Jill started to scream uncontrollably.

Her attention had been focused on Lee and she had failed to see J. T. Boswell's bloody blue arm and hand lying on the office floor. She was walking toward her desk when she stepped on it.

She had never screamed so loud before in her life.

———

As usual, the Leeco truck terminal grounds were clean and neat. Marcus Lee was a stickler for organization, cleanliness, and consistent maintenance. He had a crew constantly keeping the lawn and shrubs manicured.

The terminal sat on ten acres in the southeastern suburbs of Dallas. The terminal docks, offices, and driver's lounge were in a sprawling red brick building that covered two acres. The entire area was fenced with ten-foot-high chain link security fencing.

Leeco's common carrier routes were unusual, with a northwest run and a northeast route. No other independent in the Dallas area had ICC authority to make those runs except J. T. Boswell Trucking Company. Lee would bring freight in from major points south of Dallas, including Galveston and Brownsville, for distribution into the mainstream of America.

Marc parked the Ram 4 × 4 in the employee's parking

lot. They entered the building through a dockside door, bypassing the receptionist in the front office. Marc had spent two years of his life on that dock moving freight from one truck to another just after high school. He was glad to join the army and get some rest. Dock work was grueling. After two years of moving freight, basic training seemed easy.

The two men, dressed in western boots, denim jeans, and flannel shirts, walked into the outer office where Jill Lanier sat at her desk. She looked up, startled.

"Marc—it's good to see you. We saw you on the news the other day," she said quickly and somewhat reservedly.

"How have you been? It's been a long time," Marc said.

"I've been fine. We've all missed you."

"Is Dad in?"

"Yes, does he know you're coming?"

"Yes and no. He isn't expecting me here. Oh, this is my friend, Carl Browne," Marc said. "And Carl, this is Jill Lanier. We're old friends."

Carl Browne immediately suspected there was more to the friendship. "How do you do, ma'am?" He and Jill shook hands.

"Marc, there's something I think I should tell you before you go in there."

"What?"

"Two days ago, one of our trucks exploded in Idaho. It killed the driver—Dale Upton—you remember him. Then, yesterday, two men came in and threatened your father." She told him what had happened to Boswell, growing more upset as she spoke. "Marc, I'm really worried about your dad. Those two men blew up Dale's truck. I think it must be Mafia or something."

"Has he told Mom?"

"Probably not. You know how stubborn and proud he is."

"What else did these men say?"

"They said they'd be back at eight o'clock tonight."

"Okay, Jill. Thanks. You can stop worrying. The old man

can take care of himself. And if he needs a little help, we'll be here."

"Damn, Marc. You sound just like him."

"You know how the saying goes: Like father, like son. That's how it is. But thanks anyway."

"I just thought you would like to know. I'll tell him you're here."

"No, please. Let us surprise him. And thanks, Jill."

Marc opened the door. His dad was sitting behind his desk, running through computer printouts. When the door opened, he looked up suddenly. His face froze for an instant before he realized it was Marc.

"Hi, Dad, it's been a while."

"Marc, damn, it's good to see you," the man said as he rose from the desk. "God, boy, you look absolutely fabulous." He wrapped his arms around him in a Texas-style bear hug. "Hey, and this must be your friend Carl," he said, facing the black officer. "Howdy, Captain Browne. Welcome to Texas."

"Thank you, sir. I appreciate the invitation."

"Well, boys, have a seat and tell me what you two have been doing with yourselves. I saw you on television the other day, Marc. You looked a little tired. I guess I would be too if I'd been fightin' those sand-flea bastards like you boys. It's a damn shame you couldn't get a shot at that Qaddafi character while you were over there."

"Yeah, well, Dad, it doesn't always go the way we'd like it, but we're just the players. The coach is in Washington. You know how that goes; sometimes you have to just suck it in and do what has to be done. You understand that, don't you?"

"Sure do, son." A shadow passed over his gray eyes and he looked down at his desk.

"Something bothering you, Dad?"

"I'll tell you if you promise not to say anything in front of your mother. She worries too much," Lee said.

"Marc, the day before yesterday we had our first major accident in thirty-five years. One of our trucks hauling small arms primers exploded just outside of Lewiston,

Idaho. The driver, Dale Upton, died instantly and the rig was blown into a billion pieces—and I mean that literally. The only thing the Idaho Highway Patrol could identify was a small piece of the Idaho fuel sticker. Fortunately, it was the section with the number on it. That's how they knew who to notify."

"Damn, Dad, I hate to hear that. But aren't those primers almost overpackaged? How could they explode?"

"Damned if I know, son. There wasn't enough left to investigate the cause. So, anyway, I guess I'm a little jumpy over all that."

"I'm sorry. Is there anything Carl and I can do? We're both licensed for eighteen-wheelers in the Army. We could drive yours, too, if you're short of help. Right, Carl?"

"That's right. It might be a good change for us while we're taking a break from Uncle Sam's Army. I'd love it."

"Thanks, boys, but right now there is nothing else to do. I had to notify his family and that sure was a bitter task. How do you tell kids their daddy won't be coming home ever again? Damn, it was just so unnecessary."

"Dad, I really am sorry for you and Dale's family. I know your drivers and your company safety record have always meant so much to you. But remember, if this accident has caused you some problems, Carl and I will be around for a while. If we can help in any way, please tell us. In the meantime, Mom is probably expecting all of us for supper and Carl hasn't even met her yet. What say we head on toward the ranch and see what Mom's got cooking?"

"I've heard great things about her chili, Mr. Lee," Carl said.

"That sounds great to me, son," Marcus Lee said. "And Carl, everything you've heard about Helen's chili is true. I'll tell Jill on the way out. Besides, I need to get back down here early tonight and finish off some paperwork. It seems like business problems never end."

CHAPTER THREE

"Mom, you sure outdid yourself on this meal. I haven't eaten anything this tasty since the last time I was home. Old Carl just can't make C-rations taste quite this good. Right, Carl?" Marc asked as he stretched back from the dining room table and patted himself on his full stomach with both hands.

"Man, oh, man. I'll tell you what, Mrs. Lee, I do believe you'd give my grandma a run for her money in a cookoff, if she were still alive. This sure was great," Carl replied as he wiped his mouth one final time with his napkin. "I wish you'd teach your son to cook like this. Maybe our jumps all over the world wouldn't be so drab if he could cook like you do."

"I'll have to voice thirds on that," Marcus Lee added. "Helen, with all this food it looks like you were serving some kind of farewell feast."

"I'm just glad you all liked it. And no, Marcus, it was a welcome feast, not a farewell feast. I want Carl and Marc to feel at home while they're here," Helen said.

Helen Lee was always happy to show off her culinary expertise, but her abilities ran far beyond the kitchen. In the years Marcus was building Leeco, Helen had built a successful employment agency. She had sold the business two years before and now she spent more than thirty hours each week as a volunteer in a Dallas hospice. Even at fifty-seven, she could outwork most of the volunteers who were half her age. Although her black hair had streaks of gray, her fair skin and youthful vitality made her appear fifteen years younger.

"If you folks don't mind, I'll excuse myself and get along." Marcus Lee rose from the table, kissed his wife of forty years on the cheek, and headed to the door, not really wanting or expecting any reply.

"Okay, Dad, hurry home. We'll probably be up," Marc said.

"Good-bye, honey," Helen said as she started to clear the table.

"I'll be back as soon as I can," Marcus replied as he started out of the dining room door.

"Mom, if you don't mind, I think Carl and I will take the four-by-four and ride around the ranch a little while. I'm sure there are some coyotes running around out there somewhere and Carl has never seen one," Marc said. He felt a twinge of guilt lying to his mother. He could never recall having lied to her in all his years and he really hated to start now.

"You boys just run along and enjoy your time at home. We can all sit and talk when Marcus gets home."

"Great, see you in a little while. And, Mom, thanks for a great dinner. It sure feels good to be home," Marc said.

The two Delta Force leaders left the house and got into the Dodge Ram 4 × 4. They drove out past a large wooden barn behind the huge house. Once behind the barn, they stopped and began the transition.

They stripped out of their jeans and flannel shirts, dumping their western boots. Both men dressed in solid black: black shirts, black pants, and black jump boots. They retrieved nylon web belts from the rear of the Dodge and armed themselves. Each man carried a Parker-Imai K-633 survival knife, a Beretta 92-F 9mm automatic, and several spare magazines. An accessory pack finished off the complement of hardware. Their job would be simple and heavy firepower and accessories would simply slow them down.

They were ready for the business meeting.

They left the ranch through a back access road and headed into Dallas. The night was unbelievably black. Only distant stars dotted the horizon. The moon was nowhere to be seen. The night air was unusually warm for December.

To Marc, it didn't feel much like Christmas. Although the air was warm, the darkness was chilling, probably even frightening to most people. The elite Delta warriors weren't bothered by the darkness, because Carl Browne and Marc Lee were patrons of the night. Soldiers of darkness.

The two men of war were not afraid of the night. They would become a part of the darkness and use it as a tactical advantage.

Stealth and swiftness would be their strategic weapons against an unsuspecting enemy, their medicine to combat a deadly disease.

The hoodlums who had struck Leeco Freight Lines and Marcus Lee were the enemy, the disease.

Tonight, Marc Lee and Carl Browne would be the cure.

Tonight, the mob would learn what a trucker's family was really made of.

The two Delta warriors didn't speak until they had arrived at the Leeco terminal. They moved into the parking lot with the lights off on the 4 × 4. They parked the Ram in the shadows near the loading dock, well out of sight of anyone doing a routine search of the premises. They left the truck and became a part of the night, stopping at the corner of the brick building. Marc looked at Carl and signaled silently. Then he moved around the corner onto the end of the long concrete loading dock.

Night shadows were their allies.

They maneuvered from one overhead doorway to another without a trace of detection or opposition. Finally they were secure at a side entrance door.

"Just like Grenada?" Marc asked in a soft whisper.

"Yeah, just like Grenada," Carl said.

Marc removed a tiny spring steel instrument from his accessory pack and manipulated the doorlocking mechanism. The door gave way to his steady body weight as he pushed it open. They quickly moved into the warehouse section of the terminal. With speed and precision, the two black-clad warriors moved through the warehouse, maintaining constant cover.

There was no sound inside the building. No sign of a sentry. No sign of the hoods.

So far, so good.

Marc looked at the luminous face of his watch. It was exactly nine minutes before eight o'clock.

Their timing was perfect. It was still four minutes before they would be in position to secure the office entrance and exits.

They could finally see it. The office appeared secure. There was no sound coming from within. Still no sign of the hoods.

The side door creaked open suddenly. The same door they had come in earlier in the day. A large man in a three-piece suit came in first. He had a dark complexion, was tall. He had wavy black hair and a rugged face. Looking around, he continued cautiously before being followed by another man, and then two more.

They walked straight for Jill's office, which would take them directly into Marcus Lee's private office.

The odds had changed.

Now there were four when the men of the night had expected only two.

Marc waited.

Carl Browne moved closer to the first doorway into Jill's office.

The night erupted from deathly silence into sounds of violence.

There were shouts, then exchanges of profanity and a long, pain-filled scream.

Marc Lee could tell it was his father. His muscles tensed, sending chills throughout his body. For an instant, he was stunned. In the same instant, he regained his composure. It was his cue to move in.

He hit the dockside door opposite Jill's office with a flying scissor kick. The door splintered and disappeared beneath the impact of his powerful, muscular legs thrusting their force into the center of his feet. He rolled laterally into the office beside his father's desk, used the momentum of the roll to stabilize himself, and spun back to his feet.

He couldn't see his father.

Carl Browne came flying through the door behind the enemy, screaming. He was moving in swift, fluid motions with the grace of a seasoned ballet dancer. He danced across the floor in a blur, spinning, kicking, thrusting lethal jabs with his fists, his voice emitting bloodcurdling, savage screams.

A goon reached for a weapon under his coat.

The man's arm was fractured in three places before he could complete his reaction. Carl struck first with his feet, then a chop with the heel of his hand. The man fell to the floor, shrieking in agony.

The largest of the four goons sliced air with a samurai sword. The flash of the deadly instrument streaked through the light of the room. A swish, a miss. Another swish, a chair splintering. Still another, the man stepped back, trying to control his stance. Then he moved forward again, arcing the blade violently as he tried to make little pieces of hamburger out of Marc Lee. Marc ducked. Bobbed. Weaved. Finally he lunged at the man with a hammer thrust into his enemy's neck. The man was off balance. Lee followed the thrust with a blow to the face and a kick to the groin. The intruder collapsed to the floor. Blood trickled from his mouth.

The samurai sword was stilled.

Marc kicked the weapon out of the way as another of the men tried to strike. The man obviously didn't know his limitations. He lost his balance and fell. Marc landed a foot into the side of the man's head. The man rolled into unconsciousness as blood flowed from a jagged laceration to the top and side of his head.

The fourth man came around with a sawed-off twelve-gauge shotgun. Before he could fire, a backhand from Carl sent him and the awesome weapon to the floor. As he collapsed, Marc cracked his ribs with a front snap kick. The man screamed before he succumbed to darkness.

Carl gathered weapons and searched each goon while Marc Lee ran behind the desk to check his dad.

"My God, Carl, he's unconscious," Lee said. He could

feel his stomach tighten. "He has a serious incision to his head and part of his ear is gone. That bastard with the sword must have cut him just to scare him. I'll call an ambulance. You get those midget-minds secured. We'll deal with them later."

"Done. You just take care of your father. I'll handle these wimps," Carl replied as Marc dialed the telephone.

It seemed like an eternity, but Marc finally heard the sound of sirens penetrating the Dallas night. He had checked his father's vital signs. His breathing was shallow and irregular, but his pulse was strong. Marc had stopped the bleeding from the head wound with materials from a first aid kit on the loading dock. Even in his father's unconscious state, Marc could see the evidence of a serious brain concussion.

Marcus Lee was lapsing into a coma.

By the time the first police officer and paramedic came through the demolished doors, Marc Lee had removed his pistol belt and there was no sign of the captured intruders or Carl Browne.

"I'm Officer Johnson. What happened here?" the first uniformed officer asked.

"I'm not sure," Marc said. "I came to the terminal to see my dad and this is what I found. The place was a wreck when I got here. As soon as I found Dad, I called you guys."

"What's your name?"

"Marc Lee."

"Would you mind staying here until we get a detective?"

"I'd like to go to the hospital with my dad, if that's all right."

"Sure, I understand. If the detective doesn't catch up with you at the hospital, where can you be reached?"

"At my dad's house." Marc gave the officer the address and telephone number, then left to follow the ambulance to Dallas General Hospital.

———

"Marc, how's your dad?" Carl Browne asked. He was sitting in a soft chair in a corner of the warehouse section of the terminal building when Marc Lee walked in. It was nearly one A.M.

"He's still unconscious. I called my uncle and he's going to stay at the hospital with Mom. She's still a little hurt because we didn't tell her anything about all this going down. I guess I can't blame her." Marc was tired and worried.

"Do the doctors think he'll regain consciousness soon?"

"They're not sure. He's in a coma from the head trauma, and, of course, that's always unpredictable. His age doesn't help matters, either. How are our visitors?"

"At the moment, they're rather tied up. Come on over and see for yourself."

"You want to work it like we did in El Salvador?" Marc asked, chuckling.

"Sounds good."

The two men walked over to the corner of the warehouse section. Bruno and his three associates were indeed tied up. Carl had stripped them naked and tied each to a two-wheel dolly. The captives were standing erect on the platform of the dolly, securely bound and gagged. Stripping their clothing served a dual purpose. The men were not only relieved of any hidden weaponry, they were totally humiliated. It left Carl and Marc unquestionably in full control.

Bruno and the shotgunner, Leon, were still moaning from the excruciating pain of untended broken bones. The other two men squirmed, trying to escape the ties that bound them to their destiny.

"Well, it looks like our guests are resting comfortably, Marc. I think we should just take them over by the quarry and dump them. Maybe a single bullet in the head would do the job." Carl spoke coldly.

"I don't know just yet." Marc hesitated. "No, let's keep them a little longer. It's only Saturday morning and nobody will be back here until Monday."

"Shit, man. Let's just get rid of these creeps. They're just hemorrhoids on the ass of society."

"Let's ask them." Marc faced the naked captives. "Hey,

guys, you want to tell us a few things or do you just want me to let my friend here have his way?"

There were mumbles and grunts as the gagged and bound men squirmed in response.

"Come on, Carl. Take those gags off so these guys can have a chance to talk. Give them a break."

"I don't know, man. These bastards have done some pretty heavy shit in the last few days. I think we should just end it here once and for all." Carl looked disgusted, annoyed.

"Okay, I have a plan. Let's just take them one at a time. One gag, one man, and give them a chance. If we let the guy have a chance and he doesn't tell us what we want, you can have him and do whatever it is you do. Deal?" Marc sounded excited, happy to have recommended a compromise.

"Well, shit. I guess so. One at a time. But listen, if the mother don't talk, his ass is mine. You promise?"

"You have my word on it," Marc said. "Okay, guys, who wants to be first?"

Nobody moved. The grunts and moans ceased.

"I want that badass with the sawed-off twelve-gauge," Carl said. "I want to see how bad he is when he don't have his pants on and a big gun to make him tough."

Carl Browne started his verbal assault.

He stood directly in front of the short hood. He walked slowly around the man twice before he said a word. He looked hard at the naked man.

He placed his hands on his hips and grinned. "You know, scumbag, it ain't no wonder you carry a twelve-gauge to make you feel like a big man. If my dick was as tiny as yours, I'd carry a twenty-millimeter cannon." Browne laughed.

"Come on, Carl. Take the gag off and let the man talk."

Carl Browne removed the gag.

Leon just looked at Browne. Rage filled his eyes, but he didn't speak. He simply followed the big man with his eyes.

"You gonna answer my questions or do you wanna be the first to get a bullet, shortdick?"

"Up yours, you black son of a bitch. I ain't tellin' you nothin'."

"Oh, I see. Still a tough guy even without your twelve-gauge and your pants. Well, well." Browne shook his head from side to side as he simply looked at the floor. Suddenly he backhanded Leon squarely in the face. The man's head jerked from side to side for a second before he spoke, blood streaming from his mouth.

"You ain't shit, nigger. Your black ass is fish meat." The man inhaled deeply and spat hard into Carl's face.

Browne wiped the bloody sputum from his face with his shirtsleeve. He walked to the corner of the room and retrieved a Colt .38 Special Police Positive from a pile of confiscated weapons. He stopped and picked up a plastic container of dark brown wheel-bearing grease and walked slowly back toward the defiant hood.

"Since you still have an attitude problem, suppose I take this gun and shove it up your brave ass? You think you'd like that, shortdick? But then, from the looks of you, you're probably used to things like that."

"Your mama, nigger," the man sneered between gritted teeth.

Carl Browne gave the two-wheel a shove from the back. The rig toppled over and the little man slammed face-first into the concrete floor. Carl Browne walked up behind him, stuck the barrel of the gun into the bearing grease, and smeared the end of the barrel and the sides heavily. He leaned over and moved the cold steel barrel up and down on the crevice between the man's buttocks.

The hood jerked and twisted but he couldn't escape. He continued to mumble something. Browne noticed his buttocks tighten.

"One more chance, scumbag. You wanna talk or do I do my thing?" Browne spoke coolly and calmly now, his voice pleasant but firm.

"Screw yourself," the man said angrily, his face still pressed against the concrete floor and blood oozing from his mouth into a puddle.

"Have it your way, dude."

Browne began to insert the slender barrel of the Colt into the man's greasy rectal orifice. The frightened hood screamed, tensing with pain. Blood began to pour from beneath the gun barrel. Browne twisted it once or twice and the man screamed even louder. The scream was more of a howl, followed by pain-filled shrieks. Then, with a massive thrust, Browne crammed the barrel in all the way to the cylinder.

Marc Lee stood patiently watching, shaking his head from side to side. He said nothing for a long moment, then he spoke. "I told you guys this man likes to inflict pain. I'd reconsider my position if I were you."

Their eyes were wide in disbelief of the horror being inflicted upon their colleague. It was like looking in a mirror. These guys acted like *they* were mob.

Blood continued to flow from both ends of the defiant hoodlum. He was breathing hard and screaming at the same time. He tried to work himself free of his restraints, but every movement caused the Colt barrel to move and more pain vandalized his body.

"Last chance, shortdick. Who do you work for?" Browne asked.

"You're dead, nigger," the man grunted between tightly clinched teeth.

"Maybe so, but it'll be long after you're gone, scumbag," Browne replied. He turned his head away from the man and fingered the Colt's trigger twice. The man's body rocked as two muffled pops echoed through the warehouse.

The screaming stopped.

"Now, Marc, who do you want to give a chance to next?" he asked as he walked away from the still body with the Colt protruding from its ass.

"Damn, Carl, you've gotta stop this shit. You kill all of them and we'll never find out what we want to know. I mean, damn, guy, you just killed that son of a bitch; not that he didn't deserve it. Give them a chance. Right, guys?" he asked.

The captives tried to shake their heads in affirmation.

"I told you I just want to get rid of these scumbags. Look

at what they did to old Marcus. Now which one do you want next?"

"Well, I guess you're right. I like the big one, the one called Bruno. He sees himself as quite an accomplished swordsman."

"Sounds good to me, bro."

Browne removed Bruno's gag. The man was deathly pale. He was still staring in horror at Leon.

Fear won over loyalty.

The man started to talk.

He answered all of their questions without hesitation. Browne and Lee let him rattle on.

Bruno wasn't so big after all.

The old routine of good cop, bad cop had once more proven fruitful.

Once Marc and Carl were satisfied with the concise answers they sought, they intravenously anesthetized the men into semiconsciousness with a near overdose of sodium pentothal from their accessory packs. Carl Browne found a pair of bolt cutters and left each man with a permanent reminder of the confrontation.

Browne and Lee gathered five large wooden crates from the loading docks and uncrated the contents. Each crate was stenciled with the name BATESVILLE CASKET COMPANY.

They freed the helpless mob hardcases one at a time from their two-wheel restraints. They retied the gags and bound each man securely before loading one goon into each casket. They drilled air holes into the top of three caskets containing the three living hoodlums.

Marc Lee secured and fueled a jet-black conventional Peterbilt sleeper from the truck parking lot and attached it to a Dorsey forty-two-foot trailer. He gathered a few necessary accessories from the Dodge Ram and loaded them into the Peterbilt. He found a pair of vehicle loading ramps on the lot and attached them to the Dorsey. Then he drove the Ram 4 × 4 into the back of the trailer and secured the ramps inside. The caskets were loaded into the trailer and the Delta Force warriors headed to New York to deliver Leeco Freight Lines' counteroffer to the mob.

———

The Peterbilt rolled through the night on Interstate 40 through Arkansas and then Tennessee. It was nearly noon on Saturday before Carl stopped the rig to refuel at the Truckstops of America at Exit 374 in Oak Ridge, Tennessee. Marc had been asleep in the sleeper bay since leaving Texarkana. They decided to have a fast meal and continue on. It was only thirty-nine miles to Interstate 81 and then a straight shot to Virginia and up the Eastern Seaboard to New York.

The defeated captives lay in drug-induced sleep in the padlocked safety of the Dorsey. It would be another twenty-four hours before they would effectively regain consciousness, if they did at all.

In twelve to eighteen hours, Mafia chieftan Raffaello Segalini would have his street enforcers back.

Fortunately for society, they would be of little value to him for a long time to come.

The Delta warriors continued their journey through East Tennessee and into the Shenandoah Valley of Virginia. They stopped at White's Truck Stop in the valley for a food and fuel break. Carl bought a New York City map and they were off again.

It was nearly two A.M. Sunday when they arrived at Kings Point on the North Shore of Long Island, New York. Segalini's massive mansion was surrounded around the front by a high brick wall. From what Marc and Carl could see in the poor light, the back portion of the estate bordered the waters of Long Island Sound. Carl ran the initial recon. Marc remained with the truck a half-mile away from the mansion entrance.

Closed-circuit television constantly monitored the compound in the front and an iron gate secured the driveway entrance. Raffaello Segalini obviously lived well.

Browne returned to the truck. "Okay, Marc, just the television. There's nobody on the front gate. Bring the truck up and wait for my signal. I'll take it from there. Once the caskets are all out, haul ass."

"Sounds good to me. Let's go," Marc said.

Carl Browne jumped from the cab of the Peterbilt and sprinted back to the entrance gate to Segalini's mansion. Marc pulled the truck slowly forward. The overroad rig was out of place in the exclusive residential neighborhood—to say the least—but Marc Lee didn't plan on being there too long.

He saw the signal and slowly moved the truck in front of Segalini's gate, where he stopped the rig and jumped from the cab. Carl Browne already had the doors open on the Dorsey. They started to offload the caskets.

One by one the caskets were placed across the driveway leading into the Segalini estate.

"Carl, what about the closed-circuit television?" Marc asked as they removed the last casket.

"Hey, man, not to worry. I painted the housing lens opening black with some spray paint I found in the rig. That's my favorite color, remember?" Browne replied quickly.

"Good thinking."

"Yeah, and I think it's time to haul ass."

"Let's get at it," Marc said.

Both men climbed aboard the Peterbilt. Within five minutes they were at a pay phone miles away. Marc stopped the rig, climbed out, and went to the phone. After depositing a quarter, he dialed the private telephone number given him by Bruno. The phone rang seven times before a groggy voice answered.

"Good morning." Marc Lee spoke calmly and softly. "There's a delivery for Raffaello Segalini at the front gate. Tell the scumbag we hope he enjoys it as much as we enjoyed bringing it to him."

"What? Who is this?"

Marc Lee continued. "Tell him Leeco Freight Lines has tendered their counteroffer to his business proposition. Good day." He hung up before the voice on the other end could respond.

The real war was just beginning.

CHAPTER FOUR

"I know what time it is. You think I'm stupid? Of course I know the sun isn't even up. Just get your ass over here now." Raffaello Segalini slammed the telephone receiver back onto the cradle. He yelled to the other men in the room. "I can't believe this. Four of my best men lying in coffins. One's dead and the other three are unconscious with broken bones and their Achilles tendons cut by a bolt cutter or some such shit. I just can't believe this. What are these people, supermen or what? Listen to me, I want their nuts. Do you hear me? All of you. I want their nuts. Cut off their nuts and stuff them in their mouths. Do you understand? I'll show these bastards. One way or another, I'll show them."

"Uh, boss," one of the men said. "There was one more coffin with nobody in it. There was only this envelope. It's addressed to you." He handed the envelope to Segalini. It was a Leeco Freight Lines envelope.

Segalini opened the envelope and silently read the handwritten note. It said very simply: "The fifth casket is for you."

"What does it say, boss?" one of the associates asked.

Segalini was suddenly subdued. He handed the paper to the man, then ran his right hand through the remains of his graying hair and across a large bald spot on the top of his head. He was standing in the study of his secure mansion, but for the first time in years he was genuinely frightened.

He knew these people weren't amateurs. Only professionals could cause this kind of injury to his seasoned enforcers. Only professionals would have the balls to take on the organization.

The chieftain was dressed in a thick red velour robe, tied at the waist. He wore flat bedroom slippers that showed his real height, a slight five feet seven inches. He walked over to a huge mahogany desk and sank down in his favorite chair. He looked up at the other men in the room, and he was calm now. "Gentlemen, this is only a small trucking company we are dealing with here. Common laborers, for God's sake. It's not a friggin' army. Can someone please tell me why this family has one dead enforcer and three of our best men are permanently incapacitated?"

No one spoke.

"We were notified of J. T. Boswell's untimely demise. Why is it some redneck Texas asshole has destroyed four of my men? I have a difficult time accepting this. Has it come to the point where a good family man can no longer deal with simpletons on the level of truck drivers? The organization was built by manipulating laborers and truckers. Our unions control the bulk of the industry. Why is it that one lone independent operator can cripple the efforts of the organization? Have we become a family of weaklings?"

Again, not a man spoke. There were only blank stares.

Segalini continued. "Seventy-two hours, no more. I want the men responsible for this to appear in front of me. They can be dead or they can be alive, I don't care. I want them. Seventy-two hours, I want control of Leeco Freight Lines, with or without Marcus Lee. That little independent operation is crucial to the success of our business enterprises. Do whatever must be done. I hereby authorize a contract of one million dollars for each of the men who did this thing to our family. Bring the swine to me with their nuts in their mouths and one or more of you will be wealthy. Fail to bring them to me and I will attend each of your funerals."

———

"I think you made the right decision. There is nothing you can do at the hospital. Marcus is a strong-willed man.

He'll come out of this thing all right. And besides, you need to rest. You've been goin' for two straight days without sleep." Howard Lee looked along the side of the rural Texas road. There was nothing there except sandy, level ground dotted with mesquite trees.

"I'll go back to the hospital tonight, soon as I sleep awhile," Helen Lee replied. "I know Marcus is strong-willed. I suppose that's good. But you know, Howard, it scares me to think that Marc is exactly like his daddy. That boy is out there right now somewhere, tryin' to get to the people who did this."

"You just quit worryin' and think about gettin' some sleep. Marc can take care of himself."

Howard turned the car into the long drive leading to the Lees' home. Beyond the house lay a dark horizon, acres of fertile farmland and cattle land. The Lee ranch was an island surrounded in nearly every direction by acres of mesquite. Marcus Lee had chosen this isolated location to raise his children and retire. As it turned out, there was only one child, Marc.

He stopped the car and helped Helen to the kitchen door. She went directly to the bedroom she had shared with Marcus Lee for forty years.

"You get comfortable, Helen. I'll fix you something warm to drink and bring it up in a few minutes," Howard said.

"Thank you, Howard. You're very kind."

She already lay in her bed when Howard returned with a steaming cup of warm chocolate on a silver tray. He put the tray on a nightstand beside the bed and passed the cup and saucer to Helen.

"Thank you again, Howard," Helen said. "You know, I was just thinking about all the wonderful years Marcus and I have spent together."

"Helen, you talk about him like he's never comin' back. Like he's dead. He's gonna be okay, I promise you. It'll take more than a cut on the head to stop old Marcus."

"I'm sorry, but I'm scared, I guess."

"We all are. Don't worry, for now. Just you get yourself

some sleep and put it all out of your mind. Marcus will be back with us before you know it."

Howard left the room, made a stop in the bathroom down the hall, and retired to the study. He settled into Marcus's favorite reading chair and thumbed through a copy of *Outdoor Life*.

He saw the flash, but he never heard the sound.

The entire house was engulfed by a brilliantly blinding flash as ten cases of dynamite detonated simultaneously beneath the house.

———

Marc Lee had the black conventional Peterbilt rolling south on the Garden State Parkway. He estimated another forty miles before they reached the truckstop near Spring Lake Heights. Traffic was light as the Peterbilt roared on, sending streams of black smoke into the cold New Jersey sky.

He had his CB tuned to channel 19 to monitor other truckers. The bulk of Sunday traffic was truckers, hauling their wares across the nation. Both he and Carl were beginning to like the road. Although their journey hadn't been a typical trucker's run, they had met a lot of people on the CB as they rolled over the highways. They never divulged the true nature of their run to anyone, but they enjoyed the chit-chat on the radio. It was a distraction.

Marc remembered reading something once by a sociologist who suggested that the CB radio and truck drivers might be a new loop in human interaction, a subset of American society in which people who don't know each other manage to communicate. The writer implied that people need to communicate more freely, and truck drivers certainly had no problem with that.

There had been several times on the trip north that Marc had seen truckers helping the driver of some stranded "four-wheeler"—as they called cars. The thought of people helping others pleased Marc. There was enough hatred in the world. It was good to see something pleasant for a change. Despite all that was bad, all that was wrong with the world and society, Marc Lee knew there was still a lot of good left.

Overroad truck drivers were the new breed of cowboy—free-at-heart creatures of the wide-open spaces. Every day on the road brought new sights, new faces, and new towns. Each time a driver put blacktop behind him, he was headed to another adventure—another place—just like the adventurers of a hundred years ago. The desire to see more places, enjoy the solitude, and discover what was behind the next curve in the highway separated truckers from most of society. And for the pros, the highway was home.

Marc slowed the truck to make the exit. The truckstop was in sight. As he drove the Peterbilt into the lot, he saw another familiar sight, an LFL tractor and trailer. He figured it to be one of the drivers who always ran the northeast run and would be hauling clothing back to Dallas from New York City. The clothing manufacturing facilities always shipped a return load, Marc recalled. He could remember moving thousands of cartons of dresses and shirts on the docks at Leeco Freight.

Marc stopped the black Peterbilt across the lot from the other LFL truck. He noted it was a fairly new conventional Kenworth with a sleeper. It was painted three-tone green, with black stripes separating the shades of green along the sides. A green fiberglass Drag Foiler sat atop the big truck. The big rig glistened as the sunlight struck the shiny chrome trimmings. A pair of solid chrome smokestacks protruded from each side of the rear of the tractor's sleeper bay. The entire radiator and ventilation system on the nose of the big overroad rig was chrome. Marc couldn't help but notice that even the fuel tanks were chrome.

Marcus Lee liked his rigs to stand out on the road.

The trailer was a Fruehauf, similar to the one they had lost a few days ago in Idaho.

Marc and Carl went into the driver's lounge and asked the fuel clerk to page the driver of the other LFL rig. The driver came into the lounge a few minutes later. He was stocky with a rugged, weathered face and he was wearing a blue baseball cap with LFL on the front.

"Howdy, I'm Jim Conners. You the boys who were looking for me?"

"Thanks for coming. I'm Marc Lee and this is Carl Browne," Marc said as he stood to face the driver.

"Nice to meet you. What's on your mind?" Conners asked. And they shook hands.

"Let's get a table in the restaurant and we can talk," Carl said.

They left the lounge, found a booth in the restaurant, and sat with Conners for a long while. They explained they would be leaving their rig for a few hours for a side trip, but they avoided detailed explanation. Jim Conners agreed to keep an eye on the rig while they were gone.

The two warrior-drivers, finished a quick meal and went back out to their rig. They opened the doors on the Dorsey and removed the portable ramps. When the ramps were positioned, Carl drove the Dodge Ram 4 × 4 out of the Dorsey. The ramps were again secured inside the trailer and the double doors to the big Dorsey were locked. The men retrieved their equipment from the front of the Peterbilt and set out on their mission.

According to their maps, Ocean Grove was only fifteen miles away. Both men had committed the address to memory after Bruno had given it to them.

Carl Browne drove the 4 × 4 along the coast for five miles before they found the cross street. They made a right turn and cruised past the designated address once before stopping a block away. There had only been two cars in the drive of the oceanfront house. Both men secured the equipment they anticipated needing for the job. Each carried a silenced Uzi 9mm submachine gun, a Beretta 92-F 9mm auto pistol, and a Parker-Imai K-633 surgical steel survival knife. The pistols and the knives were attached to nylon web utility belts and fastened around their waists. A nylon musette bag, slung across their shoulders by a heavy strap, contained accessories and additional munitions.

It was showtime. . . .

Browne drove the 4 × 4 straight into the driveway of the dwelling. He parked, blocking any possible exit of the two vehicles already parked there. The warriors jumped from the Dodge Ram and ran to the front of the wood-sided house. They stopped at the front door. Browne, Uzi at ready and snug against his chest, hugged the front wall of the house. Lee stepped directly in front of the door and unsheathed a three-round burst from the Uzi SMG. The door lock mechanism disintegrated.

In a tuck and roll, both men entered the house. From the outside, the house had appeared as any other residence on the strip. But upon entering, Marc and Carl found the house was anything but that. All domestic furnishings were gone, and in their place stood rows of shelves and makeshift lab tables. Men in white lab jackets worked around the tables. Small Bunsen burners glowed throughout the room.

No doubt about it, this was the place Segalini's hardcases had told them about.

It was one of the mob's main crack houses—a place where raw cocaine was chemically concentrated to form the deadly, potent drug called "crack."

This was where the mainstay of the mob's dirty money originated. The main source of income—crack and cocaine.

The men inside hesitated before reacting. They were unsure whether the hitters were DEA or some brazen renegades. A lone guard came to bear with an M-16. Carl opened up with a silenced burst from the Uzi. The shooter took multiple rounds in his chest. He catapulted backwards before jackknifing forward into eternity.

Another man in a white lab coat tried to break and run. Marc tapped out a three-round burst from his 9mm Uzi. The man slammed into the wall, quivered a second, and collapsed to the floor. Still another man, brandishing a revolver, tried to escape. A double tap of three-rounders from the Uzi SMG and the manufacturer of white death found the hereafter.

A man appeared at the top of a staircase leading to the second floor of the house. His hand wielded an auto pistol.

The man tried to aim. His timing was way off. Browne dispatched him with another silent and deadly burst from the 9mm Uzi. The body spun twice before catapulting down the staircase.

Two more lab men threw their hands into the air and started screaming, "Don't shoot! Please, God, don't shoot! We just work here. Please!"

Still another man appeared foolishly brave. He stepped up from behind the row of shelves and tables with a Colt Python in his right hand. His finger never had time to work the trigger. Both warriors unleashed multiple 9mm death pellets into the man's upper torso. His body jerked violently, blood sprayed in the air, and he collapsed to the floor.

The warriors rushed the two men who still held their hands high above their heads, ordering them to lie facedown on the floor.

"How many more people are here?" Browne asked.

One of the men answered. "Just one more. In the bedroom."

Lee leveled his Uzi on the two prone figures and nodded his head. Browne took off in a run for the area he suspected to be the only bedroom in the house. He hit the door flying, rolling into the room. A lone gunner, an assault rifle of some type in his hands, met him as he came out of the roll. The man tried to fire, but Browne was too quick. The gleaming blade of the fifteen-inch Parker-Imai commando knife caught the man in the neck. The razor-sharp blade severed the man's windpipe as it lodged with the bloody point extruding through the opposite side of his neck. The gunner fell to the floor, lifeless. Browne removed the big knife and wiped the blade clean on the dead man's shirt.

Carl then ran to rejoin Marc in the lab. There were corrugated cartons neatly stacked throughout the lab. Clear plastic bags filled with white powder lined the boxes. Hard, caked substances were in trays all over the tables.

"What do you want to do with these two?" Marc asked.

"Let's leave them with a token reminder of our visit and blow this place," Browne replied.

"Please don't hurt us. We just work here. We don't deal this stuff." Tears filled the lab worker's eyes and his voice broke.

"This isn't much of a job, mister," Marc Lee said. "You're no better than the people who deal this death."

Browne struck the first man on the back of the head with the butt of the Parker-Imai. The man's body relaxed. Lee tapped the second man with the Uzi and he slipped into unconsciousness. Browne took a short-handled set of heavy bolt cutters from his musette bag while Lee removed the men's shoes. Browne leaned over the first man and placed the massive jaws of the bolt cutter around the man's ankle. He applied pressure to the handles and the jaws slammed shut with a pop. The Achilles tendon severed and blood poured out. Browne repeated the performance on the man's other foot and then did the same with the second white-clad wimp. They dragged the two men from the house and onto the sandy beach. A cool breeze blew across the water, chilling the early afternoon air.

The warriors ran back into the house and placed explosive charges around the room. They activated the digital timers and left.

They were less than a mile down the beach when the earth shook violently and the sounds of a massive explosion penetrated the afternoon.

CHAPTER FIVE

It had taken Marc Lee and Carl Browne twenty minutes to get back to the truckstop. They found Jim Conners. He had been in contact with Logan Duggar, who was working as the weekend dispatcher at the Leeco terminal in Dallas. Conners looked pale when he saw them.

"Something wrong?" Marc asked.

"Uh, Marc. I talked with the dispatcher, Logan Duggar, just after you guys left. We've lost two more trucks out west. They just blew up. Trucks, cargo, and drivers. What the hell is all this about?" The man was shaken.

"It's something that never should have happened. Some bad people have stuck their noses where they don't belong," Browne said.

"Marc, I have some real bad news. Uh, your—your—"

"What are you trying to say?" Marc interrupted. "Is it my father?"

"No, Marc. Not that. Your father is still in a coma. But, Marc—somebody blew up your daddy's house. Your mother and your uncle were in it. They're gone, Marc." The man just looked down at the floor.

Marc Lee felt his heart sink into the pit of his stomach. He felt the gastric juices begin to churn. His face drained of blood and his fingers felt numb. "No!" he screamed.

A waitress dropped her order. Other people became silent as Marc stood with his clenched fists raised helplessly heavenward. Carl tried to calm him, to offer comfort. But at a time like this, he knew words would not suffice.

"I'll leave you two alone for a few minutes," Jim Conners said. "If you'll give me the keys, I'll have your truck fueled and serviced so you can head on back down to Texas. And Marc, I'm sorry."

Carl gave the man the keys to the Peterbilt and sat down with Marc, who stared into emptiness, face in his hands, and his elbows propped on the table. His eyes were vacant, lackluster. Then, slowly, they turned to fire.

"I know how you feel, Marc. Believe me, brother, I know," Carl said. "It's something we all have to . . ." Browne stopped in midsentence, his voice lost in a deafening sound from outside. A shattering explosion rocked the truckstop. One corner of the parking lot was engulfed in flames that leaped over a hundred feet into the air.

Then there was another punishing explosion. More fire. This time an orange fireball rocketed into the Sunday sky. A tanker filled with gasoline had detonated in the heat of the first explosion.

Both men ran to the door to see the holocaust. But Carl Browne knew before he saw it.

The Peterbilt had blown into a billion pieces. So had Jim Conners.

The mob had found them.

Sirens were screaming in the distance as the men ran for the Dodge Ram. Carl grabbed a duffel bag full of equipment. He yelled at Marc, "They want both of us. If we split up, they'll have to take us separately. I'll take the other rig and meet you in Dallas. You get on back. Don't wait for me. I'll check it for explosives before I take off. Now get goin'."

"Thanks, brother. Be careful," Marc replied, glancing one more time at the blazing inferno he realized could have consumed either him or Carl.

"Hey, man, you okay?" Carl yelled.

"Yeah, I'll make it. Just get the hell out of here. See you in Dallas."

"Later, brother." Carl made a thumbs-up sign and ran for the remaining LFL truck.

Marc started the Ram and left the truckstop. As he spun from the parking lot, he reached into his duffel bag and slid the Uzi out of it. He laid the powerful weapon in the seat beside him and covered it with a green field jacket. Insurance.

———

Carl Browne ran a fast security check on the big triple-green Kenworth. He checked the wiring and the engine housing compartment. Nothing there.

Then he found it: a bundle of nine sticks of dynamite taped to a detonator cap and wired to the ignition system of the big rig. One tap on the starter and the Kenworth would have been history. Jim Conners had just been unlucky. He had been the first to start an LFL rig. Browne realized it could just as easily have been him or Marc Lee.

Browne removed the dynamite carefully. The wiring was sloppy. The work of a novice, but nonetheless effective. He disengaged the detonator cap and stored the dynamite and the cap inside the Kenworth. Conners had foolishly left the doors to the cockpit unlocked. But now Carl Browne thanked the dead man. It would save time.

Another complete check of the rig and the internal wiring didn't turn anything. Browne was ready to roll. He climbed aboard the rig and located the wires to hot-wire the starter. The diesel whined, coughed, then caught. Browne made the hot-wire harness permanent and prepared to move out. It had already taken him four precious minutes to clear the rig and get it started. It was time he would have preferred using to increase the distance between him and the bombers.

He was finally ready to roll. The fire still raged across the parking lot. Fire trucks and men were already battling the inferno. Red lights flashed everywhere. Ambulances, fire trucks, and police were all over the place. Browne knew it was time to leave.

Carl Browne eased the gearshift into groundhog first and started moving. He moved very slowly so as not to attract unnecessary attention. He reached the end of the truckstop parking lot and pulled into the stalled flow of traffic gawking at the fire.

Traffic moved at a crawl until he reached the Garden State Parkway. He passed the Parkway and stayed on Interstate 195. Mentally, he elected to travel I-195 to I-295 and then continue south until he reached Interstate 95 South at Farnhurst, Delaware. He would then stay on I-95 until he reached Washington, D.C. In Washington, I-95 and I-66 merged. I-66 would take him to I-81 and the rest would be a retrace of the route they had traveled coming north to New York.

Carl estimated three more hours to D.C. Once he had cleared Washington, he would rest easier. The population density would thin and he would be traveling through open Virginia farmland. It would be more difficult for the mob to hit him with so little cover. He constantly checked the mirrors for any sign of a tail.

He hadn't seen anything, but an internal sixth sense told him they were out there . . . somewhere.

———

It was dawn when Marc Lee arrived in Dallas. He had driven through the night, stopping only for fuel and fast food. It had given him time to think—time to formulate a plan to counter Raffaello Segalini.

He drove to the ranch. A final visit in tribute to his mother and uncle rekindled the memories he would always harbor. There was nothing there except the charred remains of what had once been his home. A blackened monument to uncontrolled evil in society. He watched the final moments of the morning sunrise unveil the savagery of mankind's greed. These evil men had killed good people for greed.

And then there was his father. A good man who had worked hard all his life to provide for his family. A loving man who had never harmed anyone. A man who loved his work and minded his own business. And there he was, lying just beyond the tentacles of death in a coma. A sleep from which the man might never return. It all seemed so unnecessary, so unjust.

There was the business: a thriving independent enterprise, a company built from the ground up by his father. Now there was no one to run it, to make the decisions that would have to be made to keep it in operation. Marc realized he knew very little about the inner workings of the trucking business. He had worked for his father twelve years ago, and the scope of his experience was manipulating a two-wheel dolly to move freight from one truck to the other. Marc understood the basic structure of the business, but he really had no knowledge of the day-to-day mechanics. He could drive a truck, follow a map. But when it came to routing, scheduling, payrolls, taxes, and capital improvements, he was lost. His expertise lay in weapons and communications. But given time, he could learn. He'd have to.

Of course, there was Jill Lanier. She had worked for his father since she graduated from high school. She probably knew as much about the business as Marcus Lee. The several office employees who had worked for the company since shortly after Marcus Lee founded it thirty-five years ago would also be helpful. Marc had resolved to sustain Leeco Freight Lines regardless of what it took. Leeco was a part of his family and he'd be damned if he would let it go under.

As he sat in the Ram and watched the sun rise over the remains of his childhood home, he thought of Carl Browne. He and Carl were a lot alike. They were really like brothers. The obvious difference between the two men was the color of their skin—and that was insignificant. Right now, life was the only thing that mattered.

He left the ranch and drove into Dallas. He arrived at the Leeco terminal before most of the employees got there. They had not yet heard the news of the bloody weekend. Soon enough they would know, but Marc wondered if they would ever understand.

He went into his father's office. The grim remnants of Friday night's fiasco were still there. The splintered doors, black fingerprint dust left behind by the Dallas police, and bloodstains on the carpet. Good blood and bad blood alike had seeped from bodies, both spilled needlessly.

Marc Lee sat in his father's chair, behind his desk. He looked around the office and he knew his life had changed forever.

He heard the door open in Jill's office. In seconds, she appeared at the office door. "My God!" she said. "What happened to this place?"

"We had a little problem in here Friday night," Marc said. "My dad is in Dallas General in a coma. He was hit in the head by one of those unwelcome visitors. It's been a bad weekend, Jill. You and I need to talk."

———

Marc Lee had never liked the antiseptic smell of hospitals. He liked it even less now. He stood beside his father's hospital bed and looked at the array of tubes, wires, and monitors in bewilderment. He could tell his father's breathing had improved and was almost normal. His color looked good, considering what he had been through. His head was wrapped in a white gauze bandage. The doctors had told him the ear would probably heal with time. They had managed to sew on the section that Bruno had severed. All and all, Marcus Lee had a pretty good chance—if and when he came out of the coma.

"Dad," Marc said. He picked up his father's limp hand. "They tell me you might be able to hear me. I hope you can. A lot of things have changed. Some people are going to pay for all this. Jill and I will take care of the business until you get back. Carl is bringing a rig back from New Jersey. He and I will square things. I promise, Dad. We'll ride shotgun—whatever it takes to make sure Leeco still travels safely on the highway. And by the way, we took care of the punks who did this to you. They will never hurt anyone else again. There's so much I want to say, but I guess I'd better be on my way. I'll be back real soon. Get better, Dad. Good-bye for now."

He placed his father's hand gently back on the bed,

walked to the other side of the intensive care room, and looked vacantly out the window. Looking, but not seeing. He could see one of Dallas's interstate highway loops just outside the window. Trucks and cars traveled freely. Traffic was as heavy as it always was on a Monday afternoon in downtown Dallas.

Marc took one final look at his father for a long moment and left the room. He stopped by the nurses' station, discussed his father's case for a few minutes, and then left to drive back to the terminal. He knew Carl Browne would be there. He knew what he had to do.

There was one more stop to make before he went to the terminal.

Marc wasn't sure whether he had avoided shock from the death of his mother or whether he was still in a state of denial. It was difficult to know she was dead and not even have a body to confirm it. His mother and uncle, gone without a trace. He had talked with Brittin Crain, the Dallas police detective in charge of the case, just after he had met with Jill Lanier. He had been unable to tell the man everything he knew, but just now the legal system would hurt more than it could help in his pursuit of cleansing justice.

There had been enough evidence to confirm that both his mother and his uncle had been in the house at the time of the explosion, but there was little else to substantiate their deaths. Marc stopped by the funeral home to make arrangements for a memorial service for them both. It seemed like so little to do in memory of someone who had meant so much to him all his life, but there was nothing else he could do. Not just now.

Marc headed back to the terminal to meet Jill and Carl. There was a lot of work to be done. A lot of debts to settle. His mind was in mental overload with the details, the thoughts. Even though he was a man accustomed to extreme life-and-death pressure, this burden was heavy on his shoulders. Unlike the problems he faced in Delta Force, this one was personal. The dead were his kin, his immediate family. It was common blood. There was a big difference.

Marc Lee parked his Ram Charger in the terminal parking lot and started into the building. He unconsciously scanned the trucks in the parking lot. As he got out of the Ram, he felt the Beretta under his shirt on the inside of his pants. It was the first time he consciously remembered having it with him since he had put it there three days ago. He went into Jill's office. She was sitting at her desk as usual. But something was wrong, he could sense it.

His first thought was more goons had come to the terminal. Instinctively, he reached for the butt of the Beretta. Just in case. He cautiously walked to the front of her desk. Her eyes had never left him from the time he had entered the office. As he got closer, he could see the tears distorting her azure eyes, sense the pain. "Jill, what is it? What's wrong?" His voice couldn't hide his anxiety.

She stared at him for a long moment. She tried to speak, but the words hung in her throat. "Marc—oh God, Marc! There was a phone call. . . ." Her voice was again cut short by tearful sobs. Her breathing was hard, in short, rapid, deliberate bursts. She was trying to say it, but not really wanting to. Trying to deny it. Then, in a sobbing, tearful burst, the words choked from her throat: "They've got Carl!"

CHAPTER SIX

Marc Lee caught his breath.

It was a time to rely on instinct and training.

His eyes met Jill's. For a fleeting instant, he felt something he hadn't felt for a long time.

"Jill, get Logan Duggar in here immediately." Lee spoke softly. He had calmed himself and forced his instincts to take control. There was no time for emotion. "I'm going to be gone for a few days. I need you here. Leeco needs you here. I'll try to stay in contact. You keep your ears to the ground and let me know everything that happens around here. Will you do that for me?"

"I'll do anything I can to help, Marc."

"Just knowing I can count on you is a big help."

"Marc, I know all of this has been a terrible shock for you. It has for all of us, but it's worse for you than anyone. I can tell how much Carl means to you." She looked at Marc with deep emotion. She, too, was remembering how it had been.

Logan Duggar entered Jill's office. He was a big man with a craggy, weathered face. His sandy hair was gilded with streaks of silver. Duggar had been with Marcus Lee for thirty-two years. He had watched Leeco Freight Lines emerge from a three-truck fleet to one of the largest independent trucking firms in Texas. Marcus channeled a great amount of the firm's responsibilities through this man's trusted hands. "You wanted to see me, Mr. Lee?" he asked.

"Logan," Marc said. "I'm going out on the road for a few days to see if I can find out what's going on with this company. I wanted to ask you to take care of everything while I'm gone. You're the only one here with enough experience to handle the operation. I'll stay in touch in the event you encounter any major problems. Can I count on you?"

"Of course you can, Mr. Lee," Duggar said.

"Thanks, Logan."

"And, sir, there's one more thing."

"Sure, what is it?"

"Try to get this mess cleared up so we can go on about our business. Would you do that?"

"Logan, that's precisely what I intend to do."

———

Carl Browne examined the small room. It was difficult to tell much about it in the dim light from the outside—and there was no source of light within. The only door was solid hardwood, well-aged, and locked from outside. The walls were stone and earth on the outside perimeter and concrete on the inside. There was a window below grade, fixed into an indentation dug out in the ground. The house was old and structurally sound. There was little air circulation and the humidity was high, causing a musty and moldy stench. The room was uncomfortably damp and cool. It reminded him of old houses he used to play in as a child in Nashville.

Escape wouldn't be impossible, but damn close to it. He could get through the window, but getting out of the indentation to ground level looked impossible. His body was simply too large. He could dig with his hands, but that would take time and he had no desire to stay in the place too long. If his captors came in to check him and found him digging, it would mean instant death.

He could occasionally hear voices through the hardwood floors above him. His keepers would be alert to any extensive movement he made, so Browne decided to give the matter more thought.

Thus far, his captors had treated him well, but he knew that could change any time. He wondered why his assailants hadn't killed him on sight. That was the usual method the mob used to deter opposition. His instincts told him he had been spared for a special reason. He wasn't sure what it was, but he felt sure he wouldn't like it.

Browne ran the events through his mind that had led him to this darkened cellar. He remembered pulling off of I-81 at a rest area. He was somewhere near Staunton, Virginia. He recalled passing the Staunton exits as he traveled south. He had suppressed his bodily urges for some time. He had watched the mirrors closely, looking for a tail, but there had been nothing unusual. He had parked the green Kenworth in the truck parking section at the rest area. He remembered going into the men's restroom and he was standing in front of the urinal when his world went black. He remembered trying to react, but every conscious effort his body could muster was useless. When he had awakened, he was in the cellar. He had seen his captors only once since he had been in the dark hole. He had checked himself for injuries. Nothing really hurt, but his muscles were unusually stiff. He finally felt with his hands the telltale signs of two pinhead-sized marks on his lower back.

Then he knew how they'd done it. They had subdued him with an electronic stun gun while he was relieving himself.

Browne castigated himself for being so careless. But even so, he had to commend his assailants for being able to take him so easily. Obviously, the goons who had taken him were better disciplined than the hoods he and Marc had demolished in Texas and New Jersey.

Browne settled back into the moment and surveyed his options.

They were few.

His captors had taken his Beretta and the Uzi, so the firepower was gone. His nylon belt with the big-bladed Parker-Imai was also gone. They had left him with little except his clothes, his boots, and his luminous watch. The captors had been thorough. They took every defensive device he had—almost. They would have to kill him to take away his karate expertise and they had left his watch. At least he still had that.

Browne sat on the cold earthen floor and removed his boots. He left his socks on and walked to the window. He looked up into the heavily overcast sky and could make out a glowing sphere behind the clouds. It was the sun. From what he could tell, the window faced east. He could see the top of a mountain rising far behind the house. Judging from the coolness of the basement and the gray overcast sky, Browne suspected snow anytime. He looked at the luminous face of the watch, pressed a small switch on the side of the custom electronic instrument, and smiled. He placed his right boot in the narrow windowsill. It wasn't ideal, but it would be better than having it remain too far below grade. Reaching inside his boot, he removed two tiny plastic sheaths from a pair of thin metallic strips. He pressed the two metal strips together, removed his hand, and grinned.

Carl sat back down on the cool, damp floor and said aloud to no one: "Come on, brother, do your thing."

———

Marc Lee was in the Leeco Freight Lines terminal parking lot. He had prepared the last spare rig for the road. The old cab-over Freightliner had more than two million miles on it, but Marcus Lee had always maintained it to perfection. It would be dependable. Marc hooked up an old Utility trailer to the rig. It wasn't in perfect condition, but it would do. He had managed to salvage a rusted pair of loading ramps to load the Dodge Ram. He would have preferred to travel in the Ram, but the rig would provide space for additional supplies. He could haul the Ram until he was near his objective and then offload it for the final insurgence.

The overroad rig was dispensable, the Ram wasn't. It contained the high-tech electronics that he would need to complete his mission. The Ram had to survive at any cost.

Marc started the engine on the Ram. He retrieved a

small lap computer from the Trukbox storage unit behind the rear seat and connected a 2,400-baud outboard modem to it. He plugged the wiring harness into a twenty-four-pin receptacle beside the Motorola speaker mounted under the Ram's dashboard. When he hit the power switch, the microcomputer screen came alive. He entered a lengthy encoding sequence and sat back as the transmit light lit on the Motorola VHF high-band radio.

The radio, coupled into a packet modem, sought out the correct signal path to give Marc the access he needed.

• He waited.

Marc's brain was working almost as fast as the computer. He was remembering everything he had been through in the past few days. It was a nightmare that wouldn't end. And now, sitting with a tiny electronic instrument in his lap—searching, seeking, hoping—it was like another, earlier nightmare. It was in Nicaragua, and Carl had disappeared on an advisory mission. He had been gone for six days on a patrol that should have lasted only two. His unit had come under fire in a remote section of Nicaraguan jungle. They had been pinned down for days, but they had averted capture. Their field-pack radio had been destroyed by a bullet, leaving them no communications. That had been the first time the new micro device had been used under actual field conditions. Much to the amazement and applause of Marc's superiors, the device had worked.

The *device*, as it had come to be called within the ranks of Delta Force, had been a Marc Lee brainstorm. It was a UHF digital transponder much like the transmitters found in aircraft which emit a beacon signal when an aircraft is downed. The unit had been designed to transmit a signal that could be received by the ComSat-D defense satellite in orbit over the Earth. Using ultra-high-tech engineering, the unit had finally been designed and made functional by some of the country's best communications engineers, who were on staff with the Defense Department. Marc had explained his desires in unit design and the engineers had delivered.

The final design of the device was incorporated into a microthin silicon chip circuit. The tiny electronic chip was then integrated into the functional works of a normal wristwatch. A second chip was molded into the tongue of a combat boot. The watch system could be activated by sending a dedicated code into the processor of the tiny microchip by using the existing buttons on the watch.

The boot version was a bit more complex and had a stronger transmitter. It was activated by pressing two metal tabs together inside the boot. The two-beacon transponder technology could be used as an error-rejection and backup system.

Marc Lee hoped Carl Browne was still alive. He also hoped the man had activated the transponders.

The computer screen flashed a rapid sequence of digital codes. A beeper sounded, signaling locked-on access to the vast top-secret military packet radio repeater system.

Marc typed a numeric string into the computer. A few seconds passed and the computer prompted Marc to enter his top-secret identification code, which he did.

The computer responded and indicated it was locked on to the ComSat-D satellite on the Echo uplink with response on the Zulu downlink frequency.

Marc scrolled the top-secret menu. There were only two other people in the United States with unlimited access to the amazing resources of the ComSat-D system. One was the president of the United States, the other was General Rogers at Delta Command. There was a third, the control operator of the Defense Force System, who could access only with permission of his superior officers, two of which were required to complete the top-secret digital code necessary to retrieve the access code.

Marc stopped the scroll on UTSEEK, the abbreviation for "UHF Transponder Seek." Marc entered another string of numeric functions. The computer screen flashed. In less than two seconds, the computer beeped a rapid digital tone and the screen flashed one word: LOCKED.

Marc entered another numeric string and instantly the

screen displayed two sets of numbers. He started typing in the question sequence.

> COORDINATE TRANSLATE: Vesuvius, Virginia
> GEOGRAPHIC: Mountainous
> HIGHWAY ACCESS: Virginia Route 56—Further translation requested?
> NO.

Marc shut the system down, disconnected the computer, and returned it to storage in the back of the Ram. He gathered a bundle of maps and looked for Virginia. When he found the map, he mumbled aloud: "Where the hell is Vesuvius, Virginia?"

———

Carl Browne heard the helicopter before it landed, but he couldn't see it through the small window. He could hear voices from the main body of the house—audible, but indistinguishable. He also heard footsteps moving hurriedly on the floor above him.

Browne put his boots on and laced them. He sat back down against the earthen wall and waited. He heard a door squeak open outside the door to his temporary prison. The squeak was immediately followed by footsteps coming down the stairway leading into the basement. Browne pretended to be asleep. He heard the lock click on the door to his tiny room, and immediately the hardwood door squeaked open.

Light flooded the room as two large men entered. Browne still pretended to sleep.

One of the men spoke abruptly. "Okay, dude, wake up and get on your feet."

Carl faked being startled and jerked to life as if he had just awakened. He stared at the two men for a long moment. One man held an Ingram MAC-10 and the other, a small automatic pistol.

"C'mon," the man said as he motioned with the Ingram. "Get your ass up. Somebody wants to see you upstairs."

Browne pretended to strain as he started to get off the floor. Suddenly he grabbed his lower right side and grimaced with pain. "What did you bastards hit me with, a damn crowbar? Shit, man, I hurt like hell. What the hell y'all doin' this to me for? I ain't done nothin' to you. I just drive a damn truck to try and make a livin'. What is this shit?"

"Shut up, nigger, and get movin' before I waste your ass," the man with the MAC-10 said. He shoved the barrel toward Carl Browne and motioned again. He was several feet away, out of Browne's effective striking range. "And you can cut that innocent crap, too. We know what you did to Bruno and the boys in Dallas. Now move nice and easy. Try any of that fancy shit and I'll ventilate you from your balls to your tonsils. Now move it!"

Browne looked hard at the man. His lips tightened and a scowl filled his angry face. His deep brown eyes transmitted hellfire as he walked toward the door. The goons circled around the room behind him, staying out of range as Browne walked. His instant mental assessment told him his ploy had worked partially. He knew a little more about just where he stood. He decided that when he made his move, the man with the Ingram would be the first one to die.

They reached the top of the stairs and entered the main floor of the old house. The musty smell disappeared when the basement door closed. Browne got his first look at the house. It was quite old and painted white. He could see the side of one wall on the outside. It was wood, typical of a rural farmhouse. He could see out onto the grounds. Mountains surrounded the house. Acres of open land formed a large yard before forests created a dense perimeter. Nothing unusual about that, he thought. But then, there was one thing that was very unusual. He could see at least a dozen greenhouses. From his vantage point, greenhouses were in neat rows in every direction.

It seemed odd to him that there were that many greenhouses on an old farm in the mountains.

They walked through the house to a large living room. The room was furnished in turn-of-the-century Victorian furniture. There was a sofa at one end of the room and parlor chairs in each corner. An oak coffee table held a kerosene lamp and end tables at each end of the sofa had brass lamps sitting on them. The floor was rough hardwood with a single rug in the center in front of a stone fireplace.

Browne saw three more armed men. One man, over six feet tall and weighing more than two hundred and fifty pounds, was holding a riot shotgun. Browne recognized it as an old Model Eleven Remington automatic. The man stepped behind Browne as every drawn weapon in the room pointed directly at the truck-driving warrior. The man jabbed the barrel of the riot gun into Browne's right kidney from behind. The impact sent sharp pains through Browne's body and caused him to stumble forward toward one of the parlor chairs.

Carl Browne kept his balance as he stumbled. He turned and shot a penetrating stare toward the goon and, at that instant, decided to kill the big man second.

The man with the Ingram spoke. "Sit down there." He gestured with the barrel of the MAC-10 again, pointing toward the parlor chair.

Browne hesitated, then obeyed.

Three men appeared at the door to the living room. One man was short and pudgy and remained one step ahead of the other two men who flanked him. He was dressed in a three-piece suit and wore an open brown topcoat. The man walked to the center of the room, surveying it as he moved. He held a pair of leather gloves in his right hand. He repeatedly slapped his open left hand with the gloves. He turned and faced Carl Browne. "So this is the man who has caused me so much trouble," he said. He walked around in a small circle in the center of the large room. "Perhaps I should introduce myself," he continued. "I am Raffaello Segalini. You have caused me a great deal of trouble in the last few days. I want to know why."

Brown didn't answer.

"Very well," Segalini continued. "If you don't care to answer my questions, that tells me you don't need your tongue. I could have it cut out of your mouth so you would never be able to speak again. Would you like that?"

Carl Browne smiled at the man.

Segalini saw the smile, but chose to ignore it.

The little man continued to stroll around the room. He maintained a steady rhythm with the gloves slapping his hand. "I have a shocking experience ready for you if you don't want to talk to me. You'll find it thrilling when you defecate and urinate all over yourself. Your muscles will constrict and your eyeballs will try to explode from their sockets as I take you to the threshold of death. And if that isn't enough, I'll make your balls swell slowly and painfully to the size of grapefruits before they rupture right between your legs. When you beg for death, I'll keep you alive. You can live with permanently distorted facial muscles and no balls. But all that isn't necessary if you'll tell me where Marc Lee is."

Browne looked at the man and laughed aloud.

Segalini became red-faced and stopped slapping the gloves.

Browne's face filled with determination. "Marc Lee," he said softly between tightly clenched teeth, "is comin' to blow your ass all the way to hell."

CHAPTER SEVEN

Marc Lee had memorized the route from Dallas to the East Coast. He felt like a professional driver because he had spent so many hours on the road. He anticipated what was around each curve and memorized the lines in the highway, even at night.

He was surprised at himself because he enjoyed driving the overroad rigs. Despite the nature of his business on each trip, he still liked the driving. He thought how it might be if he had his own rig. He could customize it and instill his own personality on the interior like so many other truckers he had seen. . . .

He let his mind wander as he sat behind the wheel of the huge eighteen-wheeler. He wondered just what he would do to mark his own identity on his rig, how he could make it an extension of his personality.

His mind slipped back a few days to a rig he had seen on the Interstate in Tennessee sometime in the last week. He remembered the rig vividly. It was a conventional Peterbilt with a sleeper. The rig was sleek, yet bold. It commanded attention on the highway. The long-nosed Peterbilt was painted light metallic lavender. A stunning array of artistic scrolls outlined the fine lines of the "Petercar," as the other truckers called them. The deep purple scrolling tastefully contrasted against the light lavender. The rig was spotlessly clean, its twin chrome stacks glittering in the sunlight. Everything on the big rig that wasn't lavender or deep purple was gleaming chrome. Marc couldn't help but notice the name of the rig, also in contrasting purple, painted beneath the driver's door. It said simply, THE PURPLE ROSE.

Marc couldn't see the driver, but he would never forget the beautiful rig. He thought the driver had class. Deep inside, Marc Lee knew Al Peterman would have been proud of the specimen of his namesake majestically rolling over the highways.

But then what would he do if he wasn't commanding Delta Force? The question puzzled him. The answer was elusive. He had invested twelve years of his life in military service. He wondered if he could put it behind him, take the experience, the training, and start a new life behind the wheel of an eighteen-wheeler. It seemed he was always killing, always chasing. It wasn't the way he had planned his life. Sure, it was true, killing became *easier* with every twitch of the trigger and every slash of the blade. But for Marc Lee, killing was never *easy*. He tried to rationalize it—to convince himself he had never killed anyone who hadn't deserved killing. The thought seemed to recur with unsympathetic frequency. But even so, killing was never pleasurable. He could recall many times when he had extinguished someone's life and he would want to vomit. He would almost become violently ill. And then there was the smell of death, a smell that defied description unless a person had experienced it. Once a human being had sensed the smell of another dead human, it would always be recognizable to him—always distinguishable. Marc Lee knew the human mind could never erase or repress the smell of death—ever.

The question of Delta Force was one both he and Carl would have to answer very soon. Right now, Marc Lee didn't know how he would answer it. Delta Force had given him opportunities he would never have experienced. It had made him a man, a responsible adult. But now, sitting behind the wheel of an eighteen-wheeler, rolling down the highways of America gave him opportunities also.

The decision would surely come if he survived this evil war. But right now he wasn't prepared to make that decision.

He had to fight this very personal war until it was over.

Carl Browne had determined one thing: Raffaello Segalini was a desperate man. Browne was strapped to a
stainless steel table, the kind he had seen in morgues or
pathology laboratories when he had brought in the dead
from other wars. Browne had made the move peacefully
from the living room to the small room in the rear of the
house. He had offered no resistance, partly out of curiosity
and partly because he had learned long ago never to
confront a loaded twelve-gauge shotgun while unarmed.
He was stripped naked and bound to the metal table by
heavy nylon straps around each leg and arm. His arms were
stretched above his head and away at a forty-five-degree
angle, then secured to the corners of the table. His legs
were spread and bound at the bottom corner of each side of
the table. An array of twisted wires were attached to his
chest and inside his thighs. From what Carl could see, the
wires were secured by elastic metallic bands. He could tell
by the pressure that the connections were tight.

Carl now understood what Segalini meant by a *shocking
experience*.

Segalini was standing over him beside the table. "I
believe this is something similar to the welcome you gave
some of my men in Dallas. Am I correct?"

"You got no style, man," Browne said, hardly moving
his lips as he spoke.

"You're being very foolish," Segalini said. "Tell me,
were you and this other fellow hired by this Marcus Lee
character? What did he do, answer your ad in *Soldier of
Fortune* or what? You two clowns are coming on like a
couple of mercenary commandos."

Carl Browne didn't answer at first. Segalini had just told
him he didn't know who he and Marc were. At this point,
that was good. "Man, I don't know what you're sayin'. Me
and my friend were just out to earn some bucks. Why were
you pickin' on that old man, anyway?" If Segalini knew very
little about him, it could supplement Browne's element of

surprise when he made his move to destroy the little bastard.

"You're good, real good. You must think I'm an idiot. I know who Marc Lee is and I know you are Carl Browne. I also know you are both soldiers visiting Texas on leave. My sources run deep. They are also quite efficient. I don't think you or Mr. Lee fully understand the complete ramifications of your actions to date. You have killed many of my people. You have disrupted my business enterprises and damaged the image of my family before my colleagues. I don't take such aggression passively. I have only one choice to rectify my standing in the eyes of my peers. I think you know what that is, Mr. Browne."

"Yeah, man, I know what that is. And you know Marc Lee won't rest until he puts a bullet right up your nose. You're a dead son of a bitch, Segalini."

"I think your cocky attitude will change quite soon, Mr. Browne." Segalini turned to one of his lieutenants and nodded.

The man stepped to a console filled with lights and switches. He flipped switches and twisted knobs. The lights in the room flickered for a few seconds and then stabilized.

"Show Mr. Browne how we gain cooperation," Segalini said.

The man at the console grinned and turned a knob.

Carl felt the current rushing through his body, a slight tingle at first. Then he started to tremble, to shake. Painful muscular spasms started and his blood veins protruded all over his body.

The man at the console twisted the knob further.

Browne's muscles tensed to the point that they felt they would explode. His breathing became rapid and hard. Then the breath wouldn't come. His chest wouldn't expand any further—it was like a giant truck was sitting on him. He convulsed on the table, violent tremors erupting through his body.

Segalini nodded. Suddenly the current stopped and Browne's body fell limp against the cold surface of the electrified table.

"What do you think of my little creation, Mr. Browne? An old doctor who used to work for me showed me how to construct it. His research indicated that one's attitude could be adjusted in direct proportion to the adjustment of the voltage level. Would you agree, Mr. Browne?"

Carl just looked at the man. His breathing was shallow and rapid. His body was still trembling from the effects of the electrical shock and his vision was blurred. He squinted his eyes and tightened his jaw until it was set in a chiseled display of anger. "Your time's coming, Segalini," he said.

Segalini nodded again. The console operator responded.

A stunning electrical surge ravaged Browne's body.

The operator turned the voltage up high and left it there for what Browne thought was hours, but in reality was only a few seconds. His body bucked upward in an arch, lurching from the electronic table and freezing that way, secured at the bottom and the top by the nylon ties. He screamed, tried to breathe, and his face was contorted in agony. A slight breath managed to enter his body and he screamed again. The screams filled the room, echoed off the white plastered walls, and returned to his ears as pain-filled cries of helpless agony.

The surge stopped and his body rocked back onto the table. Every muscle, every molecule within him, was trembling.

"Have you had enough, Mr. Browne, or would you like me to see if I can make your dick explode with the next round?" Segalini had a vacant look on his face. "Answers, Mr. Browne, or I shall take this treatment to a level of serious consequences."

Browne found the strength to force words from his throat. "Kill me if you can, but your number's still up. Bastard!"

Once more, Segalini nodded and the savage electrical current jolted Carl Browne's body. . . .

Carl hadn't felt the pain stop, but the overwhelming stench of ammonia jolted his sensory systems back to consciousness. A goon was standing over him with an ammonia inhalant crushed between his fingers and placed directly under his nostrils. The room smelled putrid with the stench of ammonia blended with fecal matter.

Segalini was standing over him again. A look of bitter determination filled his face. He looked into Carl Browne's deep brown eyes. "Enough for today, Mr. Browne. There will always be tomorrow. Yes, tomorrow we will start your day with a jolt, Mr. Browne. When your friend comes, we have a special table reserved just for him."

Carl Browne couldn't reply. His lips moved but his vocal cords could not function, no matter how hard he tried.

CHAPTER EIGHT

Carolyn Jameson, the night-shift charge nurse at Dallas General, thumbed through the patient roster for the sixth-floor west Intensive Care Unit. She was in her mid-thirties, slightly overweight, and a dedicated nurse. Her light brown hair was tied atop her head in a bun, making her appear at least five years older than she was. She sat behind a desk in the nurses' station alcove just off of the main hallway that ran through six west. She looked over her narrow black-rimmed glasses at the patient list for her section. She was on duty in thirty minutes for the seven-to-three day shift. Carolyn was always on the floor at least thirty minutes before her shift began. She used the time to familiarize herself with the patients assigned to her ICU.

"Good morning, Carolyn," said Dana Mills, the midnight-shift charge nurse. She was short, only five-three, and in her mid-twenties. She had deep auburn hair and light skin dotted with freckles. Unlike Carolyn Jameson, she was very shapely and attractive. "Are you about ready to run the roster and get my verbal updates?"

"Yes, whenever you are," Carolyn said, removing her glasses as she spoke. "What kind of night did you have on the floor?"

"Quiet," Dana replied. "Everything was routine. All the medications are on schedule and there were no major condition changes. Actually, we did very little. Kristi worked on cross-stitch most of the night and I read a book."

"How is Marcus Lee? Is he still resting comfortably?" Carolyn asked.

"Yes, nothing out of him. The monitors are all normal

and we checked him every hour until four A.M. He's still deeply comatose. Aside from that, he's normal."

"Just as I expected. I don't think he will ever regain consciousness. His age isn't in his favor. The poor old man will probably live for years like this, never seeing the light of day again."

"You're probably right. Okay, I'm ready if you are. Let's go," Dana said as she placed a chart back in the storage rack beside her desk. "I'm ready to get home and hit the sack. I'm tired."

The two charge nurses left the nurses' station and started their rounds. They went from room to room, examining the ICU patients. Marcus Lee's room was last. They entered and walked to his bed. Dana gasped and said, "Oh, my God, who is this?"

"It sure as hell isn't Marcus Lee, unless he changed races during the night," Carolyn Jameson said. "This man is black. What's going on?"

"Oh, shit," Dana Mills said. "They'll fire all of us. This is a midnight shift orderly and he's unconscious, he's drunk. All of the damned monitors are connected to him just like he's a patient. What happened to Marcus Lee?"

"I don't know, honey," Carolyn said, "but it's your problem. I've lost a few patients in my time, but never like this."

"Shit! I've had it," Dana said. "We've got to notify security and administration. Damn, this can't be happening. That poor old man can't possibly survive without these IVs. He's as good as dead. It's impossible. Comatose patients don't just disappear. How could he get out of this room?"

"Damned if I know," Carolyn said nervously. "This isn't him and he isn't in this room. I'm not sure what's going on here, but the real question is, where is Marcus Lee?"

———

Four of Segalini's men helped Carl Browne from the stainless steel table. They supported him—half dragging, half pushing—leading him into a shower located in one corner of the room. They let his naked body collapse to the floor and washed the feces from him with a garden hose.

Browne was semiconscious and every muscle in his body throbbed with intense pain. A putrid, bitter taste of copper filled his mouth and wouldn't go away. As the water sprayed against him like cold pellets, he spat and coughed, trying to rid his mouth of the unpleasant taste.

The water was icy cold and it tranquilized his aching muscles. The relief was short-lived when the water abruptly stopped. The men dragged him from the shower and onto the floor beside the electrified torture table. Browne stared toward the ceiling. His eyesight was blurred and he was unable to focus on anything for long without wandering away into a vacant, involuntary stare.

"My dear Mr. Browne," Segalini said, standing over him. "Morning is approaching and we have had a most interesting night. Unless you change your mind, we shall continue this attitude therapy tonight. Have a pleasant day."

Segalini left the room and the goons made Carl Browne dress himself. It took extreme effort, but he finally got his clothes on. One of the men put his boots on and stuffed his socks into his shirt pockets. He smiled and said, "Your tootsies might get cold." Then the man laughed.

Two goons helped Browne to his feet, supporting him. He was very unsteady, off-balance. They walked him back through the old farmhouse toward the temporary prison in the basement. Two armed men followed, one with the Ingram MAC-10 and the other carrying the twelve-gauge Remington shotgun.

Carl Browne's head wobbled limply with each step. His eyes still couldn't focus correctly, but he saw the butt of a pistol protruding from the belt of the man holding his right arm. His legs felt rubbery and his arms were unresponsive. The effects of the direct-current electrical shock had been devastating to his body's motor functions.

They reached the doorway to the steps leading to the basement. The man with the MAC-10 moved in front of them to open the door. He pulled the door open, stepped onto the first step, and switched on a light.

Carl Browne willed his legs to move. He caught the man on the steps with an awkward front snap kick. The man crashed down the steps, the MAC-10 gone from sight. Instantly the men supporting Browne reacted. They tried to force him to the floor, but he resisted. Carl heard the safety click of the twelve-gauge. He spun with every ounce of strength in his body, sending the man holding his left arm into the line of fire for the shotgun. The goon who had held his left arm was almost severed at the waist as a deafening roar filled the room. The man crashed into the open door with a mystified look across his dying face.

The second man tried to pull his pistol. Browne's right hand beat him to it as the shotgunner tried to snap off another round. Browne sidestepped; the hot lead pellets missed him and splintered the door. Browne worked the pistol's trigger while it was still in the man's pants. The bullet took out part of his abdomen and stopped tumbling near his testicles. The man spiraled to the floor, his hands going around his groin as he screamed, "He shot my dick off. Oh God, the bastard shot my dick off!"

Browne was up with the pistol now, point-firing. His vision was still distorted, his muscles acting solely out of instinct. The shotgunner caught three fatal rounds and crashed to the floor. Browne stumbled to the shotgun, took it from the dead man's grip, and crammed the pistol into his pants after thumbing on the safety. His hand wrapped around the pistol-grip of the twelve-gauge as two men came running through the door beside him, weapons drawn. A fast double burst from the old Remington auto sent both bodies sailing into the living room.

The shotgun had only two rounds remaining. The .45 auto had three—maybe four. He looked to the basement. The Ingram gunner was dead at the bottom of the steps, his head twisted at a distorted angle. The Ingram lay on the second step near the top. Browne grabbed it and thumbed off the safety.

He saw a door leading to a porch out the back of the

house. He cleared the back door. Snow was falling heavily and the ground was covered. His clothes were wet from the shower. The cold chilled him and the wind was punishing. He saw a man near one of the greenhouses a hundred feet away. He ran a zigzag pattern until he was near the man.

Browne knocked the man unconscious with the heel of his left hand. He removed the man's coat and found another Colt automatic and a long-bladed knife attached to the man's belt. He retrieved those and ran toward the mountains.

He knew it would be only seconds before Segalini's men came after him. It wouldn't be hard to track him in the snow. He needed a deterrent, something to slow them. Then he found it.

A huge liquid propane tank sat next to the back porch of the house. Browne steadied the .45 auto and dumped two quick rounds into the valve cover of the tank. The ground shook. A flash of fire rumbled into the sky in a tunnel of flames, sending pieces of shrapnel into the greenhouses.

Three armed men came running from the greenhouse nearest him. Browne unleashed the MAC-10, firing full-auto in a quick figure eight. The rushing men became falling bloody bodies as the pure white ground turned red.

Another man appeared, his silhouette etched against the blazing gas tank in a firing position. Browne dropped the Ingram on its sling and drew the Colt automatic. A single .45 round split the man's face open and crashed through his brain. The man tumbled backwards, his hands clawing his bloodied face as he hit the snow.

Carl Browne's body ached, but his mind was alert. The adrenaline rush caused him to regain some bodily functions. His instincts took full control and he ran toward the mountains—toward freedom.

The snow was getting heavier, and soon his tracks would be covered. Snow filled his boots, chilling his bare feet. The cold accentuated the residual pain from the electric shocks. He had little ammunition and his strength came strictly from raw determination. Carl Browne knew he couldn't afford a full-fledged confrontation with his enemy. He had to keep moving, put more distance between himself and Segalini. He had pushed himself beyond normal human limits, but he had to find a strategically advantageous pinnacle in the mountains. He had to find shelter from the snowstorm.

Carl Browne knew if he stopped moving, he was dead.

———

Activity on the sixth floor at Dallas General was frantic. Nurses, doctors, administrators, and clerical workers from every floor invaded the normally quiet halls of the ICU. They searched laundry rooms, storage rooms, patients' rooms, lounges, restrooms, and every cabinet on the floor large enough to conceal a human body.

The search was fruitless. Marcus Lee was gone.

The search expanded to every floor and every room of the gigantic medical facility. Still there wasn't a trace of Marcus Lee. The man had vanished.

Morris Satterlee, the hospital's chief administrator, was questioning Dana Mills and Carolyn Jameson. He was nervous and his tie was loose around his neck. The top button of his pressed white shirt was unbuttoned, leaving the collar open in disarray. What little brown hair he had was swept aside as if he had just stepped inside from a severe windstorm. Normally the tall, skinny man had a mellow voice, but now he was talking fast and abrasively. His voice was at least half an octave higher than normal.

"Damn it," he said. "I want you two nurses to understand something. This hospital has never, I repeat *never*, had a patient simply disappear without any trace or logical explanation. We have administered treatment to paupers and presidents alike, and we have never suffered an incident equal to this atrocity. How do you suggest I break the news to this man's next of kin? What shall I say—we've lost Mr. Lee? Or shall I simply tell them we've only temporarily misplaced him? Do you have a suggestion?" Satterlee paused, his arms folded across his chest. He was angry; his jawbone was prominent on his skinny face and he clenched his teeth. His face was deep red with the blood veins in his temples protruding visibly. "Do either of you have any idea what impact the news of this incident will have on our public image? Do you understand the legal ramifications of your negligence?"

Dana Mills was teary-eyed. Twin streams of black mascara plummeted down her cheeks and stained the front of her white uniform. She was speechless.

Carolyn Jameson faced the lanky man, her narrow glasses halfway down her nose and her eyes piercing over the top of them. She looked Morris Satterlee in the eyes. "Mr. Satterlee, while I respect your position in this matter, I should remind you, sir, that we are professional nurses and veterans of this hospital. If your precious hospital is more concerned about its image and the fear of litigation than it is for the health and welfare of its patients, then you, sir, may take this ICU and this hospital and cram it up your executive ass." She spun on one heel and walked away, slamming a medical chart to the floor as she left.

Satterlee was startled. No one, especially a nurse, had ever spoken to him that way. He dropped his arms, placed his hands in his pants pockets, and walked to the elevator. He had to contact Marcus Lee's next of kin as soon as he discussed the problem with the Dallas Police.

CHAPTER NINE

Marc Lee had been on I-81 in Virginia for two and a half hours. He felt the fatigue of his long journey. He hadn't stopped the truck since leaving Exit 143 on I-40 in Tennessee. He saw a sign that indicated Christiansburg, Virginia, was a few miles ahead. As he passed the Christiansburg exit, snow started falling. He thought it would be wonderful to have a white Christmas, but it still didn't seem like Christmas. Earlier he passed a conventional Kenworth with a huge three-dimensional Santa face on its grille. For a moment he had been amused and relaxed, but his mind had returned to the lethal nature of his business.

The snow fell in large flakes, sticking to the frozen surface of the highway. It was only minutes before the highway and the fields became a sea of white. The road was slippery, making travel hazardous because the old Freightliner didn't have tire chains. Visibility rapidly degenerated to near zero and traffic slowed to a crawl.

March kept his eyes on the road, traveling at less than twenty miles per hour. He was descending Christiansburg Mountain into the Roanoke Valley. The highway etched its way through the Blue Ridge Mountains and was treacherous now. Long grades demanded continuous gearshifting to keep the Freightliner in motion. The long rig was a hazard because it was so light on the rear end. Marc was hesitant to apply his brakes, fearing a sudden braking action on the steep downgrade would cause the rig to jackknife.

He had to keep the rig moving. Snow had already accumulated several inches and cars were stopping erratically.

75

The final grade was nearing, after which travel in the valley wouldn't be so dangerous. The last steep and winding grade was two miles miles long. The road weaved methodically through the valleys of the mountain's numerous appendages. Marc had the rig geared down to sixth gear, trying to stay off the brakes. He looked to his left and saw traffic southbound, ascending the mountain, had nearly stopped. Vehicles were sliding and spinning, trying to keep going, but few made it.

The Freightliner rounded the last sharp curve on the grade. Marc's feet and hands reacted the instant his eyes detected danger.

The rig had gained speed, traveling thirty miles per hour. The highway was like a sled track, slippery and treacherous. Ahead, not more than two hundred feet, a Roadway rig was jackknifed. The road was impassable. Two passenger cars had collided with the big truck. The highway was almost completely blocked. Marc could see injured people lying on the snow. People were everywhere, some holding their heads and covered in freezing blood, others limping about and helping the more seriously injured.

There was nowhere to go. There was a high embankment to the left and a steep dropoff to the right. A steel guardrail stood between the road's shoulder and the fall down the mountain.

Marc tried to slow the rig—to stop. His right had moved the gearshift, his left foot worked the clutch in double-time. He steered with his left hand, trying to keep the Freightliner under control. It started to skid. The trailer slid sideways and lost traction. He jerked the steering wheel into the skid and straightened the rig for an instant. The front tires lost traction. The rig oscillated, left, then right, the trailer squeaked and groaned from the stress of the awkward turns. He was on the left shoulder now, off the two-lane, snowpacked blacktop. The rig oscillated like the body of a snake crawling across hot sand. He steered back into the highway as the trailer skidded left.

It was less than fifty feet to impact. Marc tugged on the dual airhorn cord and fought the steering wheel to regain control. There was enough room to go between the guardrail and the rear of the jackknifed Roadway rig if his timing was just right and his trailer didn't jackknife. A miscalculation in either direction would mean death.

He geared as low as he dared; the diesel beneath the cab of the Freightliner whined and roared. Black smoke stampeded from the stacks. The rig slowed a little, to twenty miles per hour, but it felt more like sixty.

People involved in the wreck tried to get away. Marc jerked and fought the steering wheel even more. Ten feet . . . five . . . he hit the guardrail. The crushing sound of metal grinding against metal screeched through the air. The rig slid right, toward the dropoff. Marc pulled the wheel, battling for survival. The trailer fishtailed and slammed against the steel barrier. The guardrail held.

The Freightliner rocked off of its left front wheel from the impact. All steering control was gone. The jolt vibrated throughout the big rig with a deafening rumble. Metal continued to grind as the rig moved along the guardrail. Then the front tire crashed to the ground with a jarring thud, and the rig groaned louder from the unnatural stress.

Marc was almost past the Roadway rig, but the guardrail was still grinding into the metal of the Fruehauf trailer. Suddenly there was an explosion. Snow flew from beneath the rig. The entire overroad rig rocked and jolted. Jagged metal had punctured an outside tire on the rear of the Freightliner.

Marc cut hard left, chancing a jackknife as the rear of his trailer passed the wreckage and jerked a section of guardrail from the ground. The rig swerved, rocked, and then stabilized.

Marc geared up and accelerated. There was no time to stop for conversation, but at least he had made it without killing anyone.

He could check for damages later, but right now he had to keep moving as long as the rig was still rolling. Carl Browne's life depending on it. The very existence of Leeco Freight Lines depended on it.

Visibility had improved only slightly in the valley. Marc

Lee drove slowly for twenty miles. He saw a Truckstops of America sign as he approached the Troutville exit. He slowed in the right lane and got off.

The truckstop had a large parking lot with dozens of rigs sitting idle, many with puffs of dark smoke churning from their stacks while the drivers slept. Marc found a spot between two trucks and stopped. He gathered his nylon day bag, the Uzi, and his musette bag. He hid the Uzi under a denim jacket and went to the back of the trailer. Then he opened the large twin doors, set up the ramps, stored his equipment in the Ram, and drove the mighty 4 × 4 from the Fruehauf.

Marc would have a better chance in the Ram. The four-wheel-drive machine was almost unstoppable in the snow and he would certainly need its electronic technology. He assessed his firepower. He had the Uzi and spare magazines, the Beretta and a supply of spares for it, and his personal Desert Arms .357 automatic.

Marc left the truckstop. He turned onto a short stretch of U.S. 11 and 220 and found the entrance ramp to I-81 North. He estimated another hour to Vesuvius and he hoped Carl Browne was still alive.

———

It had been almost three hours since Carl Browne escaped from the old farmhouse. He made his way into the mountains in back of the house. Once or twice he came perilously close to Highway 56. Each time he turned away, electing instead to go deeper into the heavily forested mountain. Snow fell briskly, giving the forest floor a cleansing white coat. It would be a coat of betrayal if the goons down below followed his trail—and he knew they would.

Carl climbed higher into the Virginia mountains. It was slow going, the snow already over a foot deep. He knew well the dangers of traveling in mountainous country in the snow. There was the threat of frostbite and the risk of hypothermia. The white blanket covered every obstacle, shielding potential hazards. Even a miscalculated step into a covered six-inch hole could break his leg and mean certain death.

The air temperature plummeted rapidly around mid-morning. Brisk winds from the west swept the mountain face and created an extremely dangerous windchill factor. The dropping temperature caused the snow to change from cottony flakes to crystalline dust. The icy crystals stung the back of his neck as he ascended the mountain.

The coat he had stolen barely fit. Parts of his back and sides were exposed to the pelting snow. He started to chill badly and he feared his feet and hands would suffer extensive frostbite. His movement aided circulation and provided a degree of self-generated warmth, but it wasn't enough. He stopped once for a few minutes to put his socks on. His bare feet were stinging from the snow packed into his boots—they were almost numb. The socks relieved some discomfort, although neither the socks nor the boots were what he would have chosen for this kind of weather. The all-leather combat boots were great utility boots, but their usefulness in extremely cold, foul weather was limited.

Carl Browne wasn't a stranger to the adversities of snow in a hostile environment. He and Marc Lee had learned many lessons in the Falklands as military advisers to the British during the short-lived war in the southern Atlantic in 1982. Carl had learned to endure and to plan ahead. He had also learned to use the resources of nature to sustain his life. The mountains were full of functional resources, if only he could maintain some form of biological equilibrium until he could harvest them.

He trudged slowly along the snow-covered mountain-side. The crest of the mountain was just ahead. To the south he saw a long, narrow ridge jutting westward. He could see huge boulders forming a dark wall against the snow-covered ground. There was a dark opening thirty or forty feet from the top of the rock outcropping. It could be a cave, but he would have to get closer to be sure.

He crossed the top of the mountain below the crest on

the west side. If the goons had followed and found his tracks, he didn't want to present a perfectly silhouetted target. If they were following, he would have a chance to spot them before they spotted him.

Carl paused every hour to rest for three minutes. He used the time to survey his tracks and watch for the goons. There was no sign of anyone following him and that worried him. There were at least a dozen more men in the farmhouse and he had no idea how many more were working in the greenhouses. Segalini would never let him escape—he was too cunning and it was too risky.

Carl knew they would come. A sixth sense told him they were there somewhere—the same sense he had ignored two days ago on the Interstate. He wouldn't ignore it again.

He put his senses on full alert and gathered his strength. His muscles ached, but his vision had cleared remarkably. He could see and he could hear. His will to survive, to bring these people to a final justice, drove him.

Browne estimated ten or fifteen minutes to the rock outcropping. If he could get there safely, he might be able to survive. He wondered where Marc Lee was. He knew the man would have tried to find the transponder coordinates when Browne hadn't shown in Dallas. If Lee had been successful, he would be here soon. It had been almost twenty-four hours since the first emergency signals were transmitted. ComSat-D would have pinpointed him. Marc Lee would come.

Carl walked around the jutting ridge beneath the outcropping, staying at least a hundred yards from the stone wall. He walked around the end of the ridge before he climbed up the backside. The walk extended his arrival time at the top of the outcropping at least thirty minutes, but if the thugs were tracking, they would fall directly into his kill ground before they realized it.

He reached the top of the greenstone wall.

The wind had intensified. Blinding snow crystals swept through the sky on the wings of brutal gusts, stabbing at his bare face like tiny needles in flight. Visibility was drastically limited and the temperature continued to drop. Carl had scouted the face of the greenstone ledge as he walked beneath it to the foot of the ridge. There was an opening, but it was at least twenty feet down the straight dropoff.

In favorable weather gaining entry to the cave would have been a challenge, but in a blizzard it might be impossible. The cave would provide excellent security if he could reach it safely, but he wasn't sure how he was going to do it.

Carl made a visual inspection of the area surrounding the outcropping. There was a dense stand of black pines forty yards away. He started trudging toward the pines when he saw what he really needed: a wild grapevine dangling from the top of a hickory tree. He grabbed the vine and tugged on it. It gave way, but wouldn't break free. Carl resecured his grip on the vine and applied all his strength and weight to it.

It broke and the top end crashed to the snow-covered ground with a whisper. He coiled the vine in a roll and slung it over his shoulder opposite the MAC-10.

When he reached the stand of pines, he dropped the vine and pulled the liberated knife from its waistband sheath. It was the first time he had really looked at the knife. It was a Buck Pathfinder. It was of good quality but, like his boots, it wasn't what he would have chosen for this type of operation. He would have preferred the big Parker-Imai.

Carl cut pine boughs and piled them in a stack beside the grapevine. When he had cut all he could carry, he set out for the face of the wall.

He was again atop the stone ledge. He was shivering violently and the thought of a sanctuary twenty feet below inspired him to hurry. He located a large narrow rock deeply embedded on one end into the crest of the ridge. The other end stood three feet from the surface of the snow. The rock was two feet in diameter and it assured him of a stable base. He tied the grapevine to the bottom of the rock, made two or three turns around it, knotted it securely, and uncoiled the vine toward the face of the ledge. He buried the vine in the snow for added security.

Once it was no longer visible, he applied all of his weight to the loose end and tugged as hard as he could.

The vine held and he tossed the coil over the side of the ledge. He secured the pine bough with small salvaged pieces of the grapevine. He formed the pine and grapevine into a backpack, secured the grapevine around his waist with a slip knot, and started the climb to safety.

Carl Browne's aching hands loosely gripped the improvised lifeline as he stepped over the edge of the cliff. He moved carefully and slowly, taking one small step at a time. His feet slipped against patchy snow that had accumulated on the rock face. His muscles throbbed, but he was determined.

Five feet to go. Carl stepped even slower as the wind pressed his body against the rock wall.

He made the final plunge and his feet landed on the opening. He cautiously eased forward into the mouth of the cave. He loosened the lifeline from his waist and rewound the vine. He laid the coil just inside the cave and drew his .45 automatic.

The cave was larger then he had expected. Although the opening was no more than four feet high, once he was inside he was able to stand without difficulty. Snow had blown into the cave for two or three feet, but beyond that there was no accumulation. It was ideal. It shielded him from the elements and gave him a strategically advantageous defense point.

Carl removed the makeshift backpack and started to manufacture a torch. He took small, thick sections of the evergreen bough, tied them tightly together with tiny pieces of grapevine, and secured the bundle to a three-foot limb from the makeshift backpack frame. He smeared the boughs with as much resin as he could gather from the cut pieces of pine. He had found a plastic butane cigarette lighter in the pocket of the coat. He struck it and set fire to the pine torch.

The cave came alive, revealing a room as large as a Fruehauf trailer. It wound to his left toward the crest of the mountain. He detected a slight draft, and smoke from the boughs spiraled toward a tiny shaft at the end of the large room. Much to his surprise, there were three large half-burned logs lying amid a pile of ashes in one corner of the cave.

He wasn't the first man to seek refuge here.

There was air flow and the smoke drifted aimlessly into the earth. Carl guessed it would wind through the shaft a great distance before appearing on the surface—if it appeared at all.

Carl walked toward the mouth of the greenstone cave to gather the remaining boughs and take one final look for any goons pursuing him.

There was no sign of pursuit and that bothered him more now than ever. He couldn't figure what Segalini was up to, but he knew they would come. . . .

Carl hurried back to the logs. He stacked a pile of pine boughs beneath the dry hardwood and set fire to them with the butane lighter.

His body absorbed the warmth—the smell of burning pine and hickory was pleasant. He held his freezing hands over the blaze and rubbed them together to stimulate circulation. The stiffness dissipated and his fingers were soon limber. He warmed his front and then his backside, alternating to spread the lifesaving heat. He carefully watched the smoke to be sure it didn't flow toward the mouth of the cave.

Carl closed his eyes and leaned his head back with his chin high to stretch his neck muscles. He relaxed as his body responded to the first comfortable thing he had experienced in many hours.

Carl Browne savored the warmth and mentally planned his counteroffensive. But first, he needed to rest.

It had taken Marc Lee over two hours, instead of the hour he had estimated, to get to Exit 54 on I-81. The snow was falling in windblown sheets of tiny crystalline particles. The Ram had been in four-wheel drive since he got on I-81.

It had performed flawlessly, moving through the heavy snow like an army tank.

He was glad he had planned ahead as he drove into the twenty-acre parking lot at White's 76 Truckstop. The lot was a maze of eighteen-wheel rigs. There was hardly enough space to maneuver the Ram between the rows of parked overroad rigs. Marc kept examining each rig, hoping for some clue to Carl Browne's whereabouts.

He found nothing.

Marc stopped the Ram at the edge of the parking lot. He assembled the lap computer and entered numeric codes until ComSat-D granted him unlimited access. He entered the coded sequence for mapping Carl's personal transponder. The system went into search mode. Several seconds passed and the screen replied: NOT FOUND.

Marc tried again, reentering the sequence. Again the computer had the same response.

Marc punched the keys, new coded sequences, seeking a new identification mode. He entered Carl's transponder ID number and waited. In less than three seconds, the machine replied. Marc brought a menu to the screen and typed in the question: Time of transmission termination?

The computer replied: thirty-two minutes, seventeen seconds, eighteen seconds, nineteen seconds . . .

Marc entered: Coordinates at time of transmission termination?

The computer answered.

Marc reached to his left wrist and triggered his own transponder. He entered a sequence of digits into the computer. The screen replied: QUESTION?

Marc entered: COMPARE COORDINATES.

The computer responded.

Marc asked the machine to translate the distance to land miles.

The computer replied: 3.2652 miles east-east-southeast.

Marc immediately looked behind him. Through the snow, he could barely distinguish the dark image of a mountain crest lying directly east-southeast.

Carl Browne was somewhere on that mountain, but why had his transponder stopped transmitting?

Marc disassembled the computer and placed it in its storage compartment. He retrieved a pair of Gore-Tex Thinsulate TreBark camouflage coveralls and his LaCrosse Winnipeg boots. He stepped from the Ram and climbed into the coveralls. Once back inside the vehicle, he changed his boots. He gathered his firepower and placed everything he could carry into the pouches of his nylon web belt. He ran a check of each weapon to see that a round was chambered and all of the spare magazines were in his nylon musette bag.

Marc turned onto Highway 56. It was but a short distance to Vesuvius. Even without the blinding snow, it would have been difficult to see the little community. There was nothing there except a small country store, a wooden frame post office building, and a railroad track.

The snow was deep. There was more than a foot on the ground, but the Ram plowed through without difficulty. He continued on Highway 56, looking for anything abnormal, anything that might point the final direction to Carl Browne.

He could see nothing unusual.

He kept driving slowly, scanning the surrounding snow-covered land.

Still nothing.

Then he saw it—a large farmhouse flanked by at least a dozen greenhouses. That in itself wasn't too extraordinary. The helicopter sitting idle in the snow beside the old house was. There were three large eighteen-wheel rigs parked beside the greenhouses. For a plant farmer, that too would not be unusual. A look through Marc's binoculars gave the final verdict: two of the rigs belonged to the J. T. Boswell Trucking Company.

CHAPTER TEN

Raffaello Segalini was nervous.

"Boss," Anthony Johnson said. "The man can't be too far. This weather would kill an Eskimo. It looks like it may break outside before too long. When it does, we'll get the chopper up and find him."

"Yes," Segalini said, his voice soft. "And just what are you going to do with him once you have found him?"

"We'll take care of him, boss," Anthony said. "We still have fifteen men working the greenhouses. Shit, this guy is nothin' but a damn truck driver, he can't take all of us. Face it, the bastard's probably frozen stiff out there in the woods somewhere. He can't be alive in this weather."

"You underestimate him. This man is more than a truck driver. He is a professional killer. No one could have learned to fight like him sitting behind the wheel of a tractor-trailer. This man is a soldier first."

"We have several M-16's stowed away in the barn. I'll be sure every man has one. When we go get the son of a bitch, we'll shred his ass like pasta. He ain't gettin' away again."

"You must be reasonable, Anthony," Segalini said. "This man and his partner have caused havoc to our enterprises. We have had to stop our shipments—the plants are no longer flowing from Central America. We have enough supply left for a week, maybe ten days, then we start losing business. We showed our cards when we tried to take over Boswell and Leeco. They were the final uncontrollable link from the source to the street—and so far, we've failed to take control. Marc Lee won't let this thing rest. His mother is dead and his father is in a coma. I'm afraid we have seriously underestimated the competition. Our stoolie in Dallas is scared shitless. That is something we must remedy just as soon as Marc Lee and his black friend are deceased. It's all blown out of proportion, but we have to get rid of Marc Lee and Carl Browne. Their knowledge of our operation has left us no other option."

"Boss, these guys can't run forever."

"Anthony, I am not interested in idle conversation. I am interested in seeing these two vermin exterminated so we can continue our supply line. It costs our enterprises over ten million dollars a week when we have no supply. I, for one, have no desire to go back to working whores for a living. How about you, Anthony?"

"No, boss. I don't either."

"Our business is not safe until these men are lying on a slab with their balls in their mouths. Do I make myself clear?"

"Yes you do, boss. We'll get the chopper in the air soon and take care of Carl Browne. When we find the other one, his ass is over, too."

"Very well, do something with all the bodies. We can't have them lying around here. Do whatever you can to get rid of them."

"They need to be buried, boss. Every man deserves a decent burial. We ain't gonna be able to do it in this snow. Maybe we should take 'em back to New York and do it proper like."

"Whatever, just get them out of sight until the weather clears."

"Uh, Mr. Segalini, excuse me." Another man entered the room. "The pilot says he thinks he can fly now. Might be a little risky, but he says he can try it. He's still nervous over those mountain updrafts in this wind, but he says we'll try."

"Very well," Segalini replied. "Anthony, get those M-16's. Issue one to every man on the premises. Leave a couple here in the house and bring in a few cans of ammo. If Browne isn't dead, the crazy bastard might get brave."

"Right, boss. And we ought to have heat back in here in a little while. The mother blew the LP tank out back. One of the technicians is runnin' a line from the tanks that supply the greenhouses. It shouldn't be much longer."

"Good, Anthony. It's starting to get cold in here. Keep the fires going in all of the fireplaces until that is completed. When I get this man on my special table again, he'll never get up alive. For my sake, I hope he hasn't frozen to death. I want to be there to watch him die."

———

Even with the draft flowing through the cave, the temperature was bearable. Carl Browne had removed the confiscated coat and made a makeshift pillow. He had arranged the remaining pine boughs to provide a comfortable bed which would retain his body heat. He had laid by the fire and absorbed the warmth. His body had been ravaged, brutalized, and it needed rest. He hadn't slept in over twenty-four hours and the lack of sleep had dulled his senses. He also needed food, but that could come later. Right now, rest was the most important thing. With rest, his strength would return and his instinctive reflexes would be perceptive. When the goons came, he wanted to be ready for them. When Marc Lee came, he wanted to be able to finish this war—it all required rest.

It hadn't taken long for Carl Browne to slip into a peaceful sleep, but then the sound startled him. It echoed through the cave with deafening resonance and abruptly ended his rest.

It was loud, roaring, and much too close.

The high-pitched sound pulsated against the earth in dull harmonic reverberations.

Carl Browne had heard it thousands of times before—a helicopter.

He jumped from his cozy fireside nook. He had the MAC-10 in his right hand, a .45 auto in his left. He ran to the entrance of the cave. He didn't go too close to the mouth. Instead, he stayed a few feet back in the safety of the darkness.

The snow had stopped falling. The wind had diminished, but snow still blew from the powdery layer covering the ground. His tracks were gone, covered by drifting snow. That was a welcome edge.

Carl heard the chopper, but he couldn't see it. It had to be the mobsters, and if Segalini had men in the air, there would be men on the ground.

He inspected the perimeters of his kill zone. Nothing moved.

He mentally mapped his strategy for the kill zone if the goons came in on foot.

The chopper passed and the sound faded away. It had crossed the crest of the mountain and was searching the other side.

Then the pulsating sound returned. The chopper made another pass over the greenstone ridge and Carl Browne's cave. Again it faded into the afternoon sky and he couldn't hear it anymore.

Carl went back to the fire and retrieved the coat. The wind was still brisk and the cold had quickly penetrated his light clothing as he stood near the cave entrance. He wanted to remain out of sight, but he also wanted a clear field of view just in case some of the goons got lucky and stumbled upon him.

Browne wondered where Marc Lee was, why he hadn't gotten there. He knew his transponder signal would have been lost to the ComSat-D earth-orbiting satellite when he entered the cave. The dense rock would have attenuated the beacon transmission so drastically it couldn't possible reach the satellite.

Browne formulated his plan. If Marc hadn't shown by nightfall, he decided to make a go of it on his own. The goons wouldn't expect him to hit them. The element of surprise should counterbalance at least some of the odds. If he could strike hard enough and fast enough, he could inflict irreparable injury to the remaining hoodlums. But there were some problems—his ammunition was very limited and his clothing was grossly inadequate for the weather.

He sat ten feet inside the cave, watching, waiting, and planning. Nothing moved in the snow. The forest was quiet, desolate. It would be dark in a couple of hours—his darkness—his home. He could utilize the secrecy of the night, become a part of it, and strike with astounding effectiveness.

He wondered where the Kenworth was. What had happened to his equipment, the Uzi, his field belt, and the handheld radios? If the ComSat handheld portable radio fell into Segalini's hands, there could be big trouble. It would take the mobsters awhile to decipher the access function sequences, but General Rogers would not be a happy man.

He had to get his equipment back.

He thought about the Mafia compound. He still wasn't sure what they were doing with the greenhouses or why Leeco was so important to them. Whatever it was, Segalini seemed eager to kill for it and to allow his men to die for it.

It had been fifteen minutes since the chopper had dissolved into the sky. The perimeter around the cave was still desolate and quiet. Carl suspected the goons wouldn't want to be in the mountains in darkness. They would probably start back to the compound.

That thought quickly vanished as the Delta warrior saw the first trail bike an instant before he heard it.

The Honda off-road machine was headed straight toward the rock outcropping and his cave.

Carl could see an automatic assault rifle cradled across the handlebar of the machine. It was a M-16. The rider zigzagged between trees and deadfall, snow flying high in his wake. The rider wore a helmet and goggles, the kind Browne had seen used in dirt bike motocross racing. The man was proficient with his machine, sliding, skidding, and then continually uprighting the bike as he plowed through the snow toward Browne's sanctuary.

Carl Browne thumbed off the safety on the Ingram and then the .45 auto. He fell prone on the cave floor, his head up just enough to give him a line of sight into the forest. He waited.

If the biker didn't know he was in the cave, he didn't want to reveal his position. If he did, he wanted all the edge he could get. Presenting a smaller, less defined target was a start.

The snow-covered forest floor was over a hundred feet below him. It gave him the advantage of elevation and a better line of sight. It would be difficult, if not impossible, to spot him against the darkened rock surface. It would be harder still for the biker to hit him from the ground.

He started his mental timing and watched the undrawn outer perimeter line. He steadied the Ingram MAC-10, waiting for the biker to cross the kill line. He kept the Ingram sights, inadequate as they were, drawn on the man. Snow splayed in the air, flying in the wake of the bike as it closed the distance between them.

The bike was quiet in the snow. The fine powder muffled the sound to the point of a sporadic hum against the sounds of the wind barking through the hardwood trees.

The biker kept coming and Carl held the Ingram sights to his profile. Carl's right index finger rested against the trigger, curved in a slight arch, waiting for the right moment to touch off the first deadly round.

Without warning, the biker skidded to a stop in the snow, dropped his bike, and jumped behind the cover of dense white oak trees. In the time it took the bike to fall in the snow, the gunner was up, running.

The mountain came alive with gunfire—three-round bursts followed by full-auto fire from the gunner's M-16. The .223 projectiles slammed against the greenstone rock and disintegrated. Bullets flew wildly, splattering against the rock, sending chips of the ancient stone into the air and then to the ground below.

Carl waited, his head down, his eyes shielded from shattering lead and flying rock chips.

The gunner charged past the mental perimeter, into Carl's plane of fire. He dumped his M-16, changed sticks, and continued firing. The bullets still slammed harmlessly into the rock wall, the gunner closing fast.

Carl raised his head slightly. The Ingram sights aligned

on the gunner. Carl hesitated, not wanting to reveal his exact position.

An auto burst leveled at the cave mouth sent bullets ricocheting throughout the cave. The tiny projectiles sizzled at ultrahigh velocity into the darkness, and then splattered into harmless lead vapor.

Carl held his fire, smothered his instincts, and waited to choose his shots.

The gunner kept coming, a hundred feet from the wall now. Snow was up to his knees and running was hard. He stopped behind a tree. An empty thirty-round magazine fell into the snow. Then the gunner was out again, spraying the cave with short auto bursts.

Carl held his sights on the man. A broad smile filled his face. "Good-bye, shithead," he mumbled under his breath and squeezed the Ingram's trigger. The submachine gun rocked backwards in recoil. Three hot pieces of 9mm brass pelted the floor beside him. Tiny red dots appeared on the gunner's chest. The man spun backwards and fell into the snow, his assault rifle silent.

Carl depressed the magazine release on the Ingram and visually checked the stick. There were only ten rounds left. He did the same with the old Colt .45 auto. He counted four rounds through the witness holes. He replaced both magazines and checked to be sure each still held a round in the chamber.

Sixteen rounds . . . every shot would have to count.

Carl decided to use the bike and the M-16. Hopefully the biker hadn't burnt all of his spare ammo. Carl would kill the enemy with their own weapons and Leeco Freight Lines would again be free to run the highways of America.

His confidence was short-lived.

A small chip of rock followed instantly by heavy flying snow flew by the mouth of the cave. Another gunner, an M-16 slung over his shoulder and a revolver on his hip, plunged into the cave. A quick foot thrust and Carl Browne's Ingram and .45 automatic were gone from sight. The man was off his ropes, kicking and charging into Carl Browne before he could react. Carl fell backwards into the dark cave. The giant silhouette shrouded him, his outline visible only by the contrasting light from the mouth of the cave. The man struck hard and fast; a flying scissor kick landed with bone-crushing accuracy into Carl's side.

Carl felt an intense burning pain as his ribs snapped.

The man pivoted, flying again, this time for the head. Carl sidestepped, ducked. The man reeled, a ninety-degree pivot, and sent another foot thrust toward Carl. Carl spun again, the pain making his breathing come hard. His legs flew out with deadly accuracy, catching the man on the head. The man fell and stumbled to the stone floor. Then he was up again, his motions smooth and determined. Carl spun, a full three-sixty, and struck with a roundhouse kick across the man's face. The man grimaced with pain but kept coming. Carl threw a full foot thrust into the man's groin. The man fell and grabbed his testicles. Carl struck again, the Buck Pathfinder suddenly in his hands. The man rolled and tried to get away. Carl leaped and snapped a kick, the heel of his foot smashing the man's face. Blood flowed red and slick onto the dark cave floor. Then, before Carl could move, the man was up again, brandishing a section of burning log in his hands. Carl ducked, sidestepped, and slashed the man with the Buck. The man yelled, "You black mother . . ."

The man charged, swinging the burning log like a savage caveman. Carl lunged, countering the charge, the Buck extended from his hand. The knife found flesh and plunged into vital organs as it struck the man's solar plexus.

Carl found the M-16 and took a Model 19 Smith & Wesson .357 revolver from the body. He found two extra thirty-round sticks for the assault rifle and two speed loaders for the Smith. He wiped the blade clean on the man's bloody coat and said, "Thanks for the rope, asshole."

———

Marc Lee moved in close to the old farmhouse. The TreBark camo blended in perfectly with the landscape. When he stopped moving near a hardwood tree, he became part of the inanimate surroundings. He watched the chopper fly off and then return later. He watched two armed men leave the greenhouses on trail bikes, but he hadn't seem them return.

The Boswell trucks convinced him this was the place. The coincidence was too overwhelming, and greenhouse farmers didn't run around with M-16's.

The trek through heavy snow had been tiring, but Marc attributed part of his fatigue to the fact that he hadn't slept in over twenty-four hours. His recognition of fatigue alerted his senses even more and caused him to become overly cautious.

Marc calculated it would be another forty-five minutes until night swallowed the mountains. He found a position east of the greenhouses in the woods behind an old rough-hewn wooden barn. Although the snow had stopped falling over two hours ago, the sky was still matted with dense, heavy clouds. The night would be terribly dark. And that, Marc Lee thought, would be to his advantage.

Marc heard two men talking. When he saw them, they were walking slowly toward the old barn. One man was smoking a cigarette and casually blowing the smoke skyward. The warm, gray smoke blended with the frigid air and sailed across the opening separating him and the men. Marc could smell the smoke and hear the conversation.

"I bet the guys on the bikes find him," the man with the cigarette said.

"I can't understand why the chopper didn't spot the son of a bitch. Maybe he's already dead and covered over by snow," the other man said as they walked casually toward the barn.

"Well, either way, that bastard is one dead nigger when the boss gets his hands on him again."

"I'll just be glad when this shit is over. I want to get back to Long Island where people ain't so damn crazy."

"I can dig that. All this crap gives me the creeps. I just want to get all the goods loaded and get the hell out of here."

"Yeah, me too. That black mother's like a one-man

army, and they say the dude he hangs around with is worse than he is. Hell, just look at what they did to Bruno."

"Yeah, shit. They may be badasses, all right, but they ain't so bad this baby can't smoke their butts," the cigarette smoker said as he patted the receiver of his M-16.

Both men laughed.

They passed Marc Lee and were standing with their backs to him, oblivious to his presence, the distance not more than ten feet.

Marc had heard enough. "Kiss it good-bye, prickface," he said, closing the ground between them, the gleaming fifteen-inch Park-Imai in his extended right hand. In three solid strides the big man reached the cigarette smoker. Marc's left hand encircled the man's chin, arching it backwards. In the same swift motion, his right hand raked the huge, surgically sharp blade across the man's exposed throat. The body sagged lifelessly, leaving a gaping hole where the man's larynx had been only a heartbeat before.

The second man, too scared to scream and too surprised to run, fumbled frantically, trying to find the safety on his M-16.

He was much too slow.

Marc spun, completed an underhand arch with the Parker-Imai. The razor blade caught the man in the right kidney as Lee swung around behind him and covered his mouth. Lee lifted him from the ground at the end of the awesome knife, then let him collapse slowly.

Marc dragged the two men into the edge of the forest. He covered their bodies with mounds of snow after he retrieved their weapons. He cut a small branch from a young sapling and covered the bloody snow until there was no evidence of the fracas remaining.

He ran into an open door at the back of the barn, away from the farmhouse and greenhouses. He stopped in his tracks, dropped the Uzi to his side, stunned—it was the Kenworth that Carl Browne had driven. The doors were open on the trailer and all of the cargo was gone. Marc Lee stood there looking at the rig. "What the hell would the mob do with a truckload of women's clothing?" he muttered to himself.

Marc climbed up to the cab of the big conventional tractor. He got in and searched for anything that might tell him more about Carl's fate.

He checked the sleeper and found, much to his surprise, all of Carl's belongings were still intact. The nylon service belt, his Uzi, the handheld ComSat radio, even his duffel bag appeared undisturbed. Everything was there except Carl Browne.

Marc left the rig as he had found it and started looking around the barn. He needed to find a refuge until darkness came. Spotting a ladder leading up to a hayloft, he climbed to the top. It was filled with hay. On the northeast side of the loft he saw a small door. It wasn't more than three feet square, but it would make a good vantage point.

———

Raffaello Segalini was parading around the living room of the old farmhouse like a nervous expectant father outside a hospital delivery room. As he circled the room time and time again, he cautiously avoided walking through the bloodstains left there when Carl Browne had terminated two of his men. Each time he passed the bloodstains, his breathing became a little more rapid, his bitterness and hatred more pronounced. But more than anything else, seeing the bloodstained reminders of lives past stirred the fear consuming him, eating away at his mind.

"Anthony," Segalini said, calling the man from the next room. "Where are those men you sent into the mountain on the bikes? Why haven't they brought that man to me?"

"They're still up there, boss. They'll find him if he's still alive," Anthony said as he walked into the living room.

"Damn it, they'd better find him. I want that son of a bitch. . . ."

"We'll have everything packaged and ready to leave by morning. If we don't have him by then, we'll take every man we have and search until we find the prick," Anthony said confidently.

"Yes, Anthony, I'm sure you will. If the weather permits, I want to be out of this forsaken rat hole by early morning. I intend to have my breakfast as usual on the veranda at North Shore. Have him before then, Anthony."

"Trust me, we'll have him before then," Anthony said, his voice not as reassuring as his words. He turned and left the room.

Segalini continued to pace, stopping infrequently to rub his hands in front of the fire burning lazily in the open fireplace. He was alone, just as he had been most of his life. He let his mind wander away from the Virginia farm. He was thinking about snow again. As soon as this problem was resolved to his satisfaction, he would have an uninterruptible stream of virgin snow flowing from the southlands. White snow and green grass from Colombia and Mexico, filling his labs, his abundant cornucopia overflowing into the streets with joyful substances for those who chose to warp and twist their minds. Let them wallow in their own demented dream worlds, so long as his coffers continued to swell, so long as his money flowed forever. "What the hell," he said in a whisper, a smile crossing his lips. He reached for a cup of coffee from a table beside the fire. He savored the liquid as it warmed his body. He held the cup high in a private toast. "What the hell," he said again, this time laughing aloud. "Snort those lines, you crazy bastards. To snow . . . let the snow fall."

CHAPTER ELEVEN

Morris Satterlee adjusted his necktie and sat erect in his highback leather desk chair in the administration office of Dallas General Hospital. "Thank you, Anita, send the detective in, please," he said in his most dignified executive voice.

"Right away, Mr. Satterlee," the voice on the intercom replied.

It was but a few seconds until the door to his private office opened. Satterlee was surprised. The detective looked more like a Dallas Cowboy football player than a plainclothes police officer. The man stood at least six-three and probably exceeded two hundred and forty pounds with a highly developed physique that was evident even through this two-piece gray suit. The hospital administrator guessed the man's age to be no more than mid-thirties. Satterlee stood and extended his hand. He started to speak, but the big cop had already begun.

"Mr. Satterlee, howdy, I'm Brittin Crain, lieutenant of detectives with the Dallas Police Department." The voice resonated with a deep, natural Texas drawl as his right hand accepted Satterlee's outstretched hand. "I understand you have a problem, sir. How can the Dallas Police Department be of service to you?"

"I'm pleased to make your acquaintance, Lieutenant Crain," Satterlee said as he walked back around his desk and flexed his hand. The big detective had quite a grip. He motioned with his left hand for the lieutenant to have a seat. "Please allow me to be blunt, Lieutenant. We've lost a patient."

Brittin Crain smiled. "Well, Mr. Satterlee, don't people die in this hospital every day?"

"No, no, you misunderstood me, Lieutenant. When I say *lost*, I mean misplaced, gone."

"Maybe the patient didn't like your care and just decided to leave. You think that might be it?" Crain was still smiling.

"No, hardly." Morris Satterlee was not impressed by the detective's sense of humor. "You see, this patient was comatose. He had been injured several days ago and the man never regained consciousness. Damn it, Lieutenant, the man couldn't leave under his own power."

"I see. Well, that does present a little different picture. Who was the patient?" Crain had reverted to his low and forceful business voice.

"His name was—I should say, is—Marcus Lee. He's in the trucking business here in Dallas."

"Marcus Lee. He's the guy who got hit in the head in a robbery attempt at his terminal office. Am I right?" Crain was fishing, trying to see how much Satterlee really knew.

"I believe so."

"I tell you what, Mr. Satterlee. Do you mind if I call you Morris?"

"No, that's quite all right, Lieutenant, please do."

"Well, Morris, as I understand it, this Lee case is a delicate matter for the department right now. It's more complex than I'm at liberty to discuss. I'll go ahead and take a full report. Were there any witnesses to this man's disappearance?"

"No, none."

"All right, then . . . well, let me back off a little, Morris." Crain adjusted himself in his chair, spoke more like a detective and less like a good ole boy. "I suggest we do the report and let me handle it from there. This case has developed into a double murder and it goes on and on. I suggest you don't breathe a word of this to anyone—family, press—anyone. I want anyone who is aware of the circumstances of Mr. Lee's disappearance to do the same thing. As far as this hospital or anyone else is concerned, Marcus Lee is still a patient, his condition is unchanged, and he's still in whatever room he was in. We need to keep a lid on this for a while. Besides, it wouldn't do your hospital's public image any good to have something like this get out, would it?"

Morris Satterlee was dumbfounded. He stared at the lieutenant, speechless.

"Believe me, Morris. I think the department has a pretty good idea where Marcus Lee is. Your utmost cooperation might give us time to put some pieces together, and it just might save your missing patient's life. I can expect that cooperation, can't I, Morris?"

"Whatever you say, Lieutenant."

"Good. Now let's get that report taken care of," Crain said as he reached for a file folder. "And remember, Morris, not a word of this to anyone."

———

Carl Browne finished cutting the trouser legs off the body of the dead man in the cave. He fashioned a chest bandage from the cloth and wrapped his aching chest tightly. It relieved some of the pain from his broken ribs. The big goon had been good—but not quite good enough.

Browne slung the acquired M-16 over his left shoulder and the Ingram across his back. He put the Model 19 Smith & Wesson in his waistband on his right side and the speed loaders in his right coat pocket. He tucked the Colt .45 auto, retrieved from the man outside the greenhouse, into his waistband near the small of his back and left the chamber empty. He left the old Colt, taken from the goon he had shot in the testicles, beside the body in the cave after he salvaged the partially empty magazine. He had the Buck Pathfinder sheathed on his belt and the extra sticks for the M-16 secure in his waistband.

Carl Browne was going to war.

He stepped to the edge of the cave. The forest was black, even with the white snow covering its floor. Browne tugged on the rope used by the man who had hit him in the cave. It held.

His eyes adjusted to the darkness. He prided himself on his night vision. Marc Lee said he was half cat, able to see in the dark much better than most men. He decided it would be easier to go down the rock face than to try climbing up, since his ribs were broken.

He secured the rope around his waist and made a makeshift climbing rig. He carefully started the hundred-foot rappel down the steep stone face of the wall. It was slow and painful, every movement causing pain.

It took several minutes, but he reached the ground safely and walked to the dead biker. The man was face down in the snow and stiff from the cold. Browne rolled him over and searched his clothing. He found a small mini-Maglite flashlight in the man's coat pocket and used it to finish the search. He took gloves from the dead man's hands and put them on.

The dead man wasn't carrying a handgun, but Browne found three more thirty-round magazines for the M-16. He depressed the top round on each to be sure they were full—they were. He gathered the man's M-16 and cleared the snow from it. He depressed the magazine release, dropped the partially used cartridge holder into his free hand, and crammed a fresh stick into the well. He slapped it home and jacked a round into the chamber, then flipped the safety on and the selector lever to full-auto. He put the partially spent magazine in his left coat pocket and slung the M-16 across his free shoulder.

Browne walked to the man's bike, lifted it from the snow, and brushed off the seat. He got on and turned the ignition key. The engine fired on the first try. He revved it in neutral until it had warmed, kicked the machine into first gear, and started out through the snowy mountain forest. "I'm coming to get your ass, Segalini," he said under his breath as the bike's headlight lit the way to the killing ground.

Marc Lee watched the movement in the greenhouses for three hours. He tried to get an estimate of the mob's strength. He counted fifteen men moving through the area, but he knew there were more. Segalini obviously had a thriving enterprise in the Blue Ridge Mountain foothills, but Marc still wasn't sure exactly what they were doing. The presence of J.T. Boswell's trucks worried him. All the pieces were in plain view, but they wouldn't fit together. Before the night was over, he planned to secure the answers—and the first one was waiting in the greenhouses.

Marc climbed down from the hayloft and retrieved the two captured M-16's. He slid one across his back on the nylon sling and placed the other under a pile of hay beside the barn door. It was insurance.

He left the barn and carefully worked his way to the first well-illuminated greenhouse, seventy-five feet away. He slipped in close and checked to be sure there were no men out in the open to see him. There were none. He moved to the side of the large glass structure and tried to look inside. The glass panels were steamed over from the vast temperature contrast between the freezing air outside and the warm, humid air inside. He worked his way to the end of the greenhouse and a door. He watched for movement. He saw none. He opened the door and slipped inside, staying low in a crouch out of habit.

The extreme difference in temperature and humidity almost took his breath. The air was at least seventy degrees and the humidity felt ninety percent. The glass structure was sixty feet long. A metal frame, with side and end walls seven feet high, supported glass panels that were two feet square. The structure rose in an A-frame to an apex twelve feet from the ground. The floor was dirt, covered in sawdust. There were multiple rows of tropical plants neatly arranged on tables standing four feet off the sawdust floor. Each green plant was labeled with a colorful name tag and instructions for its care. Marc made his way through the plants, searching for anything that might tell him what Segalini was doing. Certainly the man wasn't a legitimate horticulturist.

Marc kept walking, checking each plant for a clue. He found none.

He reached the end of the greenhouse, stopped, and looked one final time at the plants. He didn't know what he was looking for, but he knew he would recognize it when he found it. He spotted a gas line coming in from outside and leading to a suspended heating unit near the top of the glass ceiling. He grabbed the aluminum gas line and cut it with the serrated top edge of the Parker-Imai survival knife. The rancid smell of liquid propane filled the air. Marc straightened the twisted tubing and let the gas escape into the air.

Lee left the greenhouse through a door on the end opposite the one he had entered. It was two large steps to another door and the next greenhouse. He could see movement midway into the structure. It was only one man. He watched through the steamed glass until the man walked away, then he bolted through the door and rolled behind the cover of the heavy foliage lining the tables. Marc moved in a crouch along the aisle parallel to the worker, separated from the man's view by the thick plants. He moved steadily until he was within ten feet of the man watering the plants.

Marc Lee stalked the man. He dropped the Uzi on its sling across his left shoulder, opting instead for the silent blade. He held the deadly knife in his right hand and found a gap in the tables just beyond the middle of the greenhouse. The man continued his work, unaware that death lurked just over his shoulders.

Marc made his move. He kept his eyes off the man and focused his attention on the water hose. He didn't want his death stare to alert the man's sixth sense. He crossed the opening and closed the gap between him and his intended victim in two giant strides.

Despite Marc's efforts, the man sensed something and turned as Marc lunged for him. The water hose fell from his hand when he saw Marc come at him with death gleaming in his right hand. The man tried to react—to scream—but the big blade finished a wide arc and slashed through his neck and esophagus before his mind could respond. The man grabbed reactively at his throat, his eyes open wide in final dismay. He collapsed, crashing into the table and knocking a half-dozen plants onto the bloody sawdust floor. As the man hit the sawdust, a potted tropical plant fell on top of his lifeless body. The pot shattered from the impact, spilling the tropical plant and the potting soil over the dead man's face.

Marc Lee froze. The first answer was right in front of him. It was lying in the dead man's face. Three clear plastic bags filled with white powder—buried beneath the plant and potting soil—had fallen into the open.

Marc picked up one of the bags, opened it, and touched his moistened finger to the fine white substance. He placed it to his tongue—it was cocaine.

Lee emptied pots, dumping the contents onto the floor. At the bottom of each pot were three bags of white powder. After he had dumped a dozen pots with the same results, he stopped. "So that's how the son of a bitch gets the stuff in here. He's importing potted plants and filling the soil with coke. Shit!"

Marc found the gas line and severed it as he had in the first greenhouse. He moved the dead man into a corner and covered him with bags of pearlite used in the potting soil. He opened the door and started to the next glass building. He heard the sound of a motorcycle coming from the forest and knew it would be one of the men he had seen leave earlier in the day. Crouching down in the corner beside the body, seeking any cover he could find, he saw the headlight as it approached a greenhouse two units from the one he was in.

He waited and heard voices as the biker came closer. Someone yelled at the man on the bike. Then, without warning, there were shots—automatic weapons fire—the rapid cycling of an M-16. He wiped the steam from the glass to get a better look. More shots came and were followed by the sound of shattering glass. The biker was moving, spinning throughout the yard. Men screamed, yelled to each other, and then there was more auto fire. The biker was headed to Marc Lee's greenhouse and bullets hammered into the fragile glass above his head.

Glass shards flew sporadically in every direction from the impact of the sizzling bullets.

Marc Lee saw the biker—it was Carl Browne.

"Give 'em hell, bro," he said and he was up, crashing through the shattered glass. The Uzi rattled hot lead into the greenhouses. Men ran wildly and sought any cover they could find.

Carl Browne circled the greenhouse, the bike doing a wheelie in the snow, then spinning and plunging back to earth. The big man screamed his blood-chilling karate scream. Men panicked and fired ineffectively at the biker— at anything. The compound was alive, bullets whizzing, auto fire chattering methodically and shattering the silent night.

Marc Lee saw lights come on all over the old farmhouse. Men in long johns ran from the house, weapons drawn. A handgun fired and was answered by the chatter of an Uzi as a man ran toward Marc. The 9mm sizzlers stopped him in his tracks and sent him into eternity.

Three gunners jumped from one of the greenhouses and fired sporadically. One man dropped to his knees and steadied his aim at Carl Browne. Marc spotted him before the man could find a sight picture. Marc's Uzi belched flaming death. The hot bullets found the man's side and rose into his head. Marc zippered the other two men with a figure eight of deadly lead. All three men collapsed into the snow.

Marc started running, bobbing and weaving, then secured cover behind the glass structure of the green-houses. It wouldn't stop a bullet, but it would hamper the enemy's line of sight. A shooter ran in front of him with his rifle chattering in Browne's direction. Marc unleashed a final burst from the Uzi. Two shots caught the man in the neck and severed it. Marc buttoned down the empty stick and crammed it into his belt. A fresh magazine almost magically appeared from his nylon musette bag and he slammed it into the well of the Israeli subgun. Lee worked the bolt back and sent a round into the chamber. A man darted from the house to Marc's right, a revolver in his hands. The man was bigger than Carl Browne. He was barefooted and dressed in thermal underwear. Marc held the subgun against his waist and fingered two three-round bursts. The man stopped instantly, jerked spasmodically, spun, and collapsed, the life gone from him.

Carl Browne did a 180-degree turn near the barn and started another pass by the greenhouses toward the old farmhouse. He passed Marc Lee and yelled, "Took you long enough to get here, brother," and he was gone, spraying .223 bullets into the glass.

A lone gunner, secure beside the corner of the house, took aim at Browne. The man fired as Browne did another wheelie. The bike flared into the air and bullets ricocheted off the frame. Browne spun his M-16 toward the man and finished off a thirty-round magazine.

Browne buttoned down the empty magazine, snatched a fresh one from his waistband, and slammed it into the assault rifle. He hammered the bolt back and let it fall as another man, armed with a shotgun, rolled from the greenhouse beside him. Browne dumped a short burst into the man and pinned him to the ground before he could finish the roll.

"Hit it, Captain!" Mark Lee yelled. "Incoming!"

Browne jumped from the motorcycle an instant before a frag grenade launched from an M-16/M-79 flashed into the gas tank. The grenade hit with a pop, flashed brilliantly, and exploded, sending the off-road machine into fragmented pieces. Brown came out of a roll, grabbed another M-16 from his shoulder, and jacked a round into its chamber. He ran laterally along the greenhouses with auto guns firing from both hands.

Marc Lee tapped a three-round burst from the Uzi and sent the frag gunner into instant eternity. He ran to the fallen man and retrieved the M-16/M79, grabbed the rifle, and dove into the greenhouse beside the body in a tuck and roll. As Marc stopped rolling on the sawdust floor, he saw a case of M-79 fragmentation grenades lying beneath a plant table. He grabbed the crate and spilled a corrugated box full of papers. They were shipping manifests, each almost

identical to the other. Every manifest was from Leeco or
J.T. Boswell's firm. Marc ducked and scanned through the
documents. Each document had two things in common: It
was consigned to Vesuvius Horticultural Research Center
and it bore one of two authorized signatures.

He had found the second piece to the puzzle.

Marc picked up the grenade crate and ran for the outer
perimeter of the farmhouse yard. He stashed the grenades
away from the action and took a half-dozen for the portable
launcher.

Marc Lee loaded a frag round into the muzzle of the
M-79. He aimed at the farmhouse and dispatched a round
into an upper floor window.

The house illuminated for an instant and then became a
fiery volcano as boards flew under the impact of the
explosion.

Marc readied another round and fired into the lower
floor of the old house. Once more an intense illumination
transformed into a blazing conflagration.

Marc's peripheral vision detected two gunners working
their way toward him. Their silhouettes were projected
against the fiery old farmhouse. The men stopped and took
cover between the cab and trailer of one of J.T. Boswell's
rigs. Marc loaded another grenade. He steadied his aim and
squeezed the round off into the fuel tank of Boswell's truck.
Diesel fuel splattered and ignited at the same instant. The
cab rocked under the force of the explosion and disintegrated. Both gunners ran screaming across the yard toward
the greenhouses. They were on fire, saturated in diesel fuel
and ignited by the fire from the grenade. They ran wildly,
black putrid smoke pouring from their burning clothing and
flesh, their arms clawing into the night, reaching for
eternity. One man ran into the greenhouse in front of the
old barn. A microinstant after he entered the structure, his
flaming body was hurled skyward by the cataclysmic explosion of liquid propane ignited by his burning clothing.

Fire from the first explosion caused the next greenhouse
to detonate. The sky illuminated with the intensity of
daylight when the second glass building ignited. Shards of

glass rained onto the killing field as men scrambled for cover.

Marc Lee ran to the case of grenades and grabbed two more. He ran to the back of the farmhouse, which was almost fully involved in flames. He sent another grenade flying into the back of the house.

Carl Browne was mopping up the farmyard. He wondered where Raffaello Segalini was.

Another greenhouse exploded.

Carl made a frantic dive for cover as the yard was again littered with sharp shards of glass.

He didn't hear the helicopter start, but he caught sight of two men as they fled the burning house. They disappeared from sight before Carl could fire. It was Raffaello Segalini, running and firing a snub-nosed revolver. Anthony Johnson was in front of him and he pulled Segalini into the helicopter as the pilot throttled the engine.

Marc Lee didn't hear the chopper until it was airborne. The roar of the burning house and the explosion had concealed the sound. He swung his M-16 toward the fleeing aircraft and dumped a full magazine. He heard a few rounds strike metal, but the skybird disappeared into the darkness.

CHAPTER TWELVE

Marc Lee was thankful it was the kind of night all normal people would be inside. The temperature was still in the low teens and the wind had started blowing again, fanning the flames of the burning old farmhouse. Flames reached into the Virginia sky several hundred feet, lighting the night around the farm. Heat was intense around the burning structure.

Even though the old farm was isolated, someone would eventually see the fire and call the local authorities.

He wanted to leave as quickly as he and Carl could.

Carl Browne opted to walk for the Dodge Ram, despite the fire burning in his rib cage. Marc gave him the keys and assembled everything they wanted to take with them. He salvaged the box of manifests from the greenhouse and placed them in the back of the Fruehauf with the crate of M-79 grenades. He gathered a dozen M-16's and threw them in also. He also salvaged two 840-round ammo cans that hadn't been touched. He grinned as he loaded them. The canisters were stenciled 5.56 BALL. It was stolen military ammo.

Marc found two full five-gallon gasoline cans in a storage room in the barn. He moved them into the yard to use just before they pulled out.

He climbed into the cab of the Kenworth and unraveled Carl's hot-wire job. He found the correct wires and started the rig. He let the diesel engine warm to temperature before he drove it from the barn. He was shocked when the rig started so easily in the intense cold, but the engine purred to perfection. He drove beyond the burning farmhouse and stopped a safe distance away, then slung his Uzi over his shoulder, checked the Beretta on his hip, and walked back to the greenhouses.

He heard Carl coming in the Ram. They located a pair of lightweight ramps which had been used, they determined, to load the motocross bikes into the back of a rig. They set the ramps up and drove the Ram into the open doors of the Fruehauf. Once it was inside, they loaded the ramps and secured the doors.

"You ready to go?" Carl asked.

"Almost," Marc said. "I found a couple cans of gasoline in the barn. Let's finish the job before we leave."

"Let's do it. Old Raffaello will be snug in bed on Long Island before we get to D.C.," Carl said as the men started walking toward the barn.

"Yeah, the superslab is in rough shape. It may take awhile."

"Superslab?" Carl asked. "Man, you're already talkin' like a truck driver. You thinkin' about not reuppin' when this leave is up?"

"I haven't decided. And you?"

"I don't know yet; twelve years of doing the same thing—it's hard to quit. You know what I mean, don't you?"

"Yeah, I sure do. But if my father doesn't come out of this coma, I can't just leave the business. I won't walk away from it. Four years is a long time when you look at how things are just now."

"Yeah, but there are some good people working for your father. They can handle things. Jill could probably run the company by herself."

"Unfortunately, old buddy, everything is not rosy in Dallas," Marc said.

"What do you mean?"

"I found some manifests in one of the greenhouses during the firefight. This whole thing's been a setup. Segalini's got somebody on the inside at Leeco. My guess is, it's been going on for years.

"Well, I'll be damned," Carl said.

The men stopped walking when they reached the

gasoline cans. Each took a can and walked through the remaining greenhouses. They saturated everything that would burn and met in the yard. Marc poured a gasoline trail from the last greenhouse. He struck a match and dropped it into the gasoline path.

In a flash the greenhouses were engulfed in flames. By Marc's best estimate, eighteen thousand packages of cocaine were going up in smoke. Marc Lee knew even Don Raffaello Segalini couldn't withstand that kind of loss.

It had been almost four hours since Marc Lee and Carl Browne boarded the Kenworth and left the bloody killing ground behind them. They had traveled I-81 to its junction with I-66 at Strasburg, Virginia. The journey hadn't been too uncomfortable. Marc slept for two hours in the sleeper bay while Carl drove the rig. The Virginia Department of Highways had done a good job of removing snow. All that remained was a light film of compressed snow. Traffic had been all but nonexistent, making travel easier. Most motorists had observed warnings issued by the news media and had avoided travel. That hadn't been possible for Carl Browne and Marc Lee.

"Hey, man, did you finally wake up?" Carl asked as Marc climbed from the sleeper.

"Boy, I sure needed the rest. How are you feeling?"

"I'm next and I sure could use some chow if you're in the mood," Carl said.

"Find us a place to stop and we can refuel this thing and eat."

"I saw a sign awhile back that said a truckstop was fifteen miles ahead. That okay with you?"

"Sounds good to me. How are your ribs?"

"It's like I've been run over by one of these rigs. They'll get better with time. I'm going to have to get back on active duty with Uncle to get any rest."

"I know. I didn't plan all of this, you know."

"I know. I'm sorry for you it all happened."

"It's a shame something can't be done to clean up this industry. There are a few bad apples out there who spoil everything for everyone—cast that lingering shadow of doubt on the industry. You follow me?"

"I know what you're saying. Most drivers and companies are on the level. They're honest. Then there are people like Segalini who jump in and use a legitimate business for their own corrupt purposes. Somebody should be able to do something; I agree."

"Well, I have to hand it to Segalini," Marc said. "The man is shrewd. He's probably been running cocaine from a pipeline in Texas for years. I mean, who would have thought to inspect every tropical plant that crossed over a loading dock?"

"But why Leeco? Why not some other company?" Carl asked.

"I'm not sure yet. Some of it makes sense and some of it doesn't. Leeco and Boswell are both common carriers for the northeast. Both companies also have western routes. I have some ideas, but I'm not completely sure why it was us."

"You think we can get anything from Segalini when we find him?" Carl asked.

"I don't know, but I plan to try. It'll be up to him. My guess is he'll die before he tells us anything."

"You may be right."

"Either way," Marc said. "I think the answer is still in Dallas. There's the exit; let's eat."

"You got it, Major. I'm starving."

Carl maneuvered the rig off the Interstate and onto the exit ramp. He turned onto a two-lane road and drove to the truckstop a mile away.

Carl stopped in the first available fuel bay. He climbed from the cab and hailed the young fuel attendant. "Top it off on both sides. We'll be inside getting a bite to eat."

"You got it, mister," the young man said.

Marc and Carl went inside the truckstop restaurant and found a table. They scanned the menu and settled for eggs, sausage, biscuits, and gravy. They sipped at cups of coffee until the waitress returned a few minutes later with their order, then assaulted their food, devouring it in minutes.

A big-screen TV was on in a corner near their table. It was CNN all-night news. Carl looked up just as the screen showed a pretty young girl reporting. The sound was barely audible over the noise in the dining room. Suddenly he saw his face on the screen—he and Marc Lee were on television.

"Brother, you better turn around real easy and look at this," Carl said.

———

Raffaello Segalini sat in the library of his estate on the North Shore of Long Island. He looked across Long Island Sound, beyond the Gold Coast to the Connecticut shoreline. The ocean water was whitecapping, rolling in the steady wind. Snow covered the grounds and disappeared at the water's edge. He could see his helicopter, tied down beside the heated pool on the back lawn of the prestigious, isolated estate.

Segalini's flight from the foothills of the Blue Ridge Mountains to the elegant North Shore had been anything but pleasant. The wind had beat the helicopter across the sky, nearly forcing the pilot to set the ship down on three different occasions. The rear stabilizer had been hit by gunfire when they took off in Virginia. The damage wasn't critical, but the controls had acted sluggish. It had created a dangerous addition to the treacherous weather.

Segalini's anger had left him, replaced by fear. He looked over the red terrazzo veranda, past the rolling water, beyond the Connecticut shoreline, and into the vast emptiness. Soon the sun would illuminate the dark clouds in the eastern sky. Darkness would be replaced by a reddish hue burning from the surface of the water into the morning sky. "An omen," he said aloud. He was alone in the library, but surrounded by fear. "How can two men—two mortal men—assault the organization and cause so much damage? This cannot be."

Segalini sat down in a Victorian highback chair. He reached for the telephone and dialed a number. The phone rang and Marzio Cavallo answered. "Marzio, please forgive me for disturbing your rest. This is Don Segalini."

"Yes, Don Segalini. What matters disturb you at this hour?" The man sounded as if he were still asleep.

"The organization is in danger, Marzio. We need your help, we need your men."

"And what is this danger, Don Segalini?"

"We are being opposed by outside sources which threaten the very thread of our existence. Two men, commandos—trained killers, the best I have ever witnessed—are coming. I fear they are coming for me, Marzio."

"I have heard of these things, Raffaello. This matter has troubled the organization's council for some days now. We have sat, Raffaello, and it is our determination that you have crossed over the undrawn line. You have brought unnecessary attention to the families, which is a source of substantial embarrassment to the organization. Just look around you, Raffaello. This is not good for the organization—it is not good for you. There is talk, Raffaello, that perhaps you haven't the zest necessary to direct the organization any longer. There is talk . . . that perhaps you should be ousted."

Raffaello Segalini sank in his chair. He paused a long moment before he responded. "It is a terrible thing, this problem. But you, Marzio, you and the others have added unexpected complications. I cannot forgive that. The council should never meet without my personal approval. I am still in charge of the organization. What you have done without my consent is traitorous. And you, Marzio, what is your feeling on this matter?"

The voice paused as a long breath came from the telephone. "Raffaello, you have always been like a father to me. You have nurtured me, protected me, and guided me in my times of torment and trouble. I would lay my life down for you as I would a brother. But this, my dear friend, is different—this war you have gotten yourself into concerns more than a pipeline and a single source; it concerns the organization. I, as well as the other family heads, fear you have fueled a fire which will burn for some time to come. We have no desire to do battle with the Federals. The heat has been off of us for years, our businesses have flourished—your business and mine. This Leeco Freight Lines is not worth sacrificing our businesses. You are a man with many troubles, Raffaello. It will be difficult for you to continue to lead our brotherhood. Perhaps, my friend, you should give this matter serious review before you continue on this course of suicide. As you, of all people, should know, it is a grave error to underestimate one's opposition . . . inside or outside of the organization."

"I see," Segalini said, and he hung up the telephone.

———

Marc Lee hit the snow-covered pavement outside the truckstop in a dead run. Carl Browne was one stride behind him. "Hey, man, you want to tell me what's going on here?" Browne asked, never breaking his stride into the snowy lot.

"Later, brother," Lee said without slowing his pace. "Right now, we've got to get to Segalini. This has to end—we have to end it. Our future and Leeco's future depend on it."

They were sixty or seventy feet from the Kenworth when a car appeared, speeding across the lot. Snow and slush splatterd in its wake. The car was spinning, the driver acting crazed. The engine roared and the rear end of the car fishtailed wildly.

Lee and Browne heard the car before they saw it.

The passenger's window opened. A man with an automatic weapon appeared from the front seat. The roaring chatter of gunfire rattled across the truckstop parking lot. Bullets ripped into the snow at Lee and Browne's feet. Snow and slush splattered against them.

The gunner couldn't control his shots because the car was moving so erratically. Another gunner appeared, this time from the rear of the dark gray Buick. The man had a

9mm automatic pistol. He, like the submachine gunner, fired sporadically, and his shots missed.

Marc Lee was out with his Desert Eagle .357 Magnum automatic. He double-actioned the first shot, pausing a short second as the metallic twang of lead meeting steel echoed across the lot. His second shot was automatic and was followed by a quick third. The Buick's windshield spiderwebbed as the car spun sideways, its rear end toward them. The driver floored the accelerator. The car spun 180 degrees and headed straight for them.

Carl Browne was out with his Beretta 92-F. He fired three fast rounds into the grille of the speeding car. Steam appeared, followed by a high-pressure misty spray of boiling water from the radiator.

The gunners were undaunted, firing constantly toward Lee and Browne. Bullets whizzed past Lee's head and caused him to dive to the ground.

Carl reached the Kenworth. He climbed up, jerked the door open, and leaped inside. He fumbled for an M-16 tucked away in the sleeper bay, jacked the bolt back, turned it loose, stripped the first round from the magazine, and allowed the round to slam into the chamber. He flipped the selector to full-auto and clicked the safety off. Without stopping his motion, he jumped from the cab on the opposite side from the one he had entered. He hit the snow and fell into a tuck and roll toward a rig parked beside the Leeco Kenworth. The roll absorbed the impact of the fall and Browne sprang to his feet with wet snow clinging to his clothing.

The car was directly in front of him now. The gunners had changed sides, firing from the opposite side as the car sped past Lee and Browne. Browne unleashed the .223 assault rifle and the bullets created a lightning stream of hot flying lead as they struck the car. Before the burst was completed, Browne was in another roll. His body splashed slushy snow as he stopped beside the front tire of an International overroad rig.

The gunners went down in the seat when the auto fire was returned. Lee was still lying in the wet snow. He jumped up when the shots from the car stopped and reached the Kenworth, following almost exactly the previous movements of Carl Browne. He, too, retrieved an M-16, jacked, stripped, and bolted from the rig. He opened fire from a crouch.

The car spun and made another pass, the driver still bravely assaulting. Gunfire was loud and penetrating.

Carl Browne was up, firing the assault rifle. He dropped it to the sling around his neck and came up with the Beretta. He rapid-fired until the Beretta was empty and the slide locked open. Browne reached for a spare and the movement caused his injured ribs to throb. He found the spare, buttoned down the empty, slipped it into his waistband, slammed the fresh stick into the grip well, and thumbed the slide lock down. The car was close. Browne dropped into a crouch, double-actioned three fast rounds, and smiled as the gunner in the backseat catapulted backwards.

One down.

The driver spun the car again, leading into another pass. The front gunner still belted out lead toward Lee and Browne, unaffected by the death of his companion.

Lee jumped directly in the path of the vehicle. He squeezed the M-16's trigger and held it tightly in a full-automatic death burst. The rounds found the front of the car and the windshield vanished into indistinguishable pieces. The driver riveted against the back of his seat as the death missiles bolted him to the upholstery and perforated his upper torso.

Two down.

The front seat gunner fired to the finish as sizzling bullets smashed his life from him a heartbeat after the driver died. His auto gun was silent and the car sped out of control.

Carl Browne and Marc Lee saw it coming. The car headed into the undercarriage of an Amoco gasoline tanker parked across the lot. The impact sheared the top from the vehicle as it wedged under the heavy tanker. A valve severed from the bottom of the tanker and created a gaping hole flooded with gasoline. The volatile substance needed only one spark.

There was a flash, and the car, tanker, and gunners became an intense orange fireball. In a microinstant, the tanker erupted like a volcano.

CHAPTER THIRTEEN

Jill Lanier thought it unusual that Marc Lee hadn't called her since he had left Dallas. What if Marc were seriously injured, or worse yet, what if he were dead? What would happen to Marcus Lee—to Leeco Freight Lines?

The mob had changed a lot of things, not the least of which was her personal feelings for life and Marc Lee.

She walked along the corridor to the administrative section of the terminal complex. She stopped at a water fountain and took a cool drink to clear her dry throat. As she stood, she caught herself speaking quietly aloud. "It shouldn't have come to this. It's all so unnecessary. All the money in the world isn't worth dying for." And she continued along the corridor, shaking her head in disbelief.

"Jill," Logan Duggar said from his office off of the corridor.

"Yes, Logan," she said, her mind returning from supposition to reality as she turned to his office door.

"Have you heard from Marc?"

"No. As a matter of fact, I was just thinking about that. He should have called by now."

"Well, he probably hasn't found anything. I hope his friend is all right."

"So do I."

"Have you checked on Marcus's condition today?"

"I called earlier this morning to see how he spent the night."

"And?"

"The nurse I spoke with said nothing has changed; he's still in a coma, but resting comfortably. Amazing, isn't it?"

"Yes, it is. I wonder if he'll ever come out of this?"

"I try not to think about that. There's been enough dying. It's time to start thinking about living."

"Maybe that's what all of this is about, Jill—living."

———

Logan Duggar tried to concentrate on a stack of shipping manifests on his desk. He thumbed through routing books and selected the best route for common carrier shipments to be transferred from the Leeco terminal. He stopped abruptly, removed his glasses, and ran his fingers through his sandy gray hair. "I still can't believe all this," he said aloud, and he cupped his head in his hands. He felt bad for Marcus Lee and for Helen. He recalled the early days, when Leeco was young, when he was young. Marcus Lee had lured him away from J. T. Boswell, and together they had worked punishing hours to build a company from three broken-down old rigs. It had been successful, but the relationship between him and Marcus had always remained businesslike. The only social contact he could remember with Marcus Lee was at annual company Christmas parties or a summer company picnic. Over the years, he asked himself why Marcus Lee always remained aloof—the answer had never come.

Logan Duggar felt he had contributed as much to the success of Leeco Freight Lines as Marcus Lee. Sure, Marcus invested the money and took the risks, but *he*, Logan, ran the company when Marcus was away, and he was *the* senior employee. He knew everything there was to know about the daily operation of Leeco. When there was a problem, he was the first one consulted. He had all of the responsibility, but little of the spoils. And then one day he awakened and realized life had all but passed him by. He wondered why he had stayed, why Marcus Lee had never offered to make him a partner. And he thought, maybe if he had, none of this would have happened. . . .

———

Jill returned to her office. She sat in front of the computer terminal and her mind wandered back through the last few days. Although her romantic relationship with Marc Lee had ended years ago, her involvement with the Lee family had flourished. Marcus Lee often called her the daughter he never had. She was like family—almost. She had always wanted to *be* family, married to Marc Lee, but now she wasn't so sure.

She tried to put it all into some logical perspective and think it through. The thoughts and the memories meshed and formed a mirage of emotional confusion. Her life had been running smoothly until Marc Lee came back into it, and now it hurt almost as much as it had when he left. "Damn you," she muttered aloud as she wiped the tears from her surreal blue eyes. "Why did you have to come into my life now? Damn you, Marc Lee."

———

It had taken nearly six more hours to reach the New Jersey coast and cross over the bridges onto Long Island. The snow had not fallen as heavily in New York as it had in the mountains of Virginia and along the coast. The storm frontal system had moved out to sea off the coast of southern New Jersey, and New York had been spared the punishment of a heavy snowfall. It would make the job a little easier.

Marc had driven most of the way, permitting Carl to sleep and get much-needed rest. The drive had been pleasant except for the constant awareness that Segalini's mob wanted them dead and police all over the coast were looking for them. The latter, in itself, created a level of stress he didn't need right now. Marc Lee had no quarrel with the law or its enforcers. In his mind, he felt he hadn't done anything wrong—had only done what any reasonable and prudent man with his ingrained abilities would have under similar circumstances. Marc Lee had killed many times before in the name of national security and democracy. Those killings were called justified, police actions.

Certainly, if killing for an ideology was justified, fatal retribution for the spilling of one's own family blood was not only justified, it was expected.

The body count in this war was high—too high. It would likely get higher before it ended. But it *was* a war—and in wars, people die. If Marc Lee could rid society of even some of the human leeches—those who prospered by the degradation of others—perhaps the lives of innocent people could be saved in the long run. Then it would all be worth it.

Early afternoon traffic on Long Island was heavy and moving slowly. Marc eased the rig through the maze of commuters, constantly watching his mirrors, looking for the next wave of hired killers. He didn't believe Raffaello Segalini would permit them to drive right into his estate without paving the way with blood. Marc expected the proverbial red carpet, but he expected the red to be blood.

Carl Browne wasn't resting comfortably. Several times over the past few hours, Marc heard the man moan in his sleep. He had been tossing and squirming in the sleeper. Carl had told him some of the details of his time with Segalini. He knew Carl was hurting from the torture inflicted by the mobster. Marc Lee was hurting too, but in a different way. Carl's pain would pass with time, soothed by his body's own rebuilding processes. But Marc wasn't sure *his* hurt would ever go away. He wasn't trying to minimize Carl's pain, but physical pain usually healed with time—mental pain possessed a tendency to linger and resurface when it was least expected.

Marc thought about reupping, staying in the military for another four years. He had devoted twelve years of his life to a military career; but then, his life was devoted to his family. He owed Marcus and Helen Lee something for their efforts in conceiving him, bearing him, and raising him. Maybe it was repayment time.

Marc couldn't remember a time of personal crisis in his life when his father hadn't been there. The relationship had always been close and open. His father worked, it seemed, all the time when he was young. Yet he had still managed to have time to devote to his son. It was time of great quality—time used to build the memories of his youth—pleasant, enjoyable memories. It was all past now, water that had flowed under the bridge of time and become lost in the torrents of life. But the stream of life flowed on, renewed with new currents, new influx, and it all swirled together to create new torrents. Somewhere along the flow, Marc thought, there had to be new eddies, places of calm where the weary could take comfort in rest and solitude.

If Marc left Delta Force, he could run Leeco. He could be an active participant, even drive a rig himself. He liked the time behind the wheel. Maybe, he thought, this *is* one of the eddies. The solitude of driving the giant overroad rig, ridding high above everything else on the road, and isolated to a world sealed within the cab of the big tractor.

It would be an option when this war was over. But then there were the Segalinis of the world. If one man had caused such havoc, Marc wondered what other evils lurked inside the trucking industry. What were the problems of men like Marcus Lee who carved a living out of rolling metal and rubber over blacktop highways? Truckers were the wheels of this nation. Moving freight was not a luxury, it was a necessity for the functional existence of the United States. Everything from bedpans to Earth-orbiting satellites had at one time or another been moved by truck. And where there was necessity, there was greed and evil, maligning the very nature of the resource. Segalini's assault had been ambitiously motivated out of insatiable greed. Despite the man's respectable facade, he was nothing more than a murderous dope runner. The man represented the residue of a sick society rotting in an abyss of chemically dependent torment—he was scum.

Marc realized the expertise possessed by he and Carl Browne could be applied to other facets of terrorism—to other rapes of innocence. Maybe, when this war ended, he and Carl could retreat to one of life's eddies and then surge back into the torrid currents, refreshed and rested, ready to bleach the doers of evil with cleansing fire and wash them from the face of decent society. It was an option.

A pain-filled cry startled Marc Lee. Carl Browne awakened from his sleep and screamed in pain.

"You all right back there, Captain?"

"Damn, man, my chest is on fire. That big bastard in the cave kicked the hell out of me. I never knew broken ribs could hurt so much."

"I know it hurts, but it'll heal."

"Yeah, it'll heal. Where are we?"

"Long Island. I figure maybe another hour or so until we need to find a place to offload."

"Let's find a place to eat. I shoot better on a full stomach."

"Are you sure you're up to this? I can go it alone. Maybe you need to rest."

"No way. I'm hurtin' like this because of what that man has done. No, I'm in for the run."

"You sure?"

"Damn right I'm sure," Carl said as he climbed through the curtain separating the sleeper from the cab. He held his side, his left arm wrapped across his chest and his face twisted with pain. "You want me to drive awhile?"

"No, I'm fine. I'll get us to a stopping place. You just rest and build up some energy. I suspect it's going to be rough when we find this creep."

Marc drove for forty-five minutes and neither of them spoke. Their attention was focused on everything around them.

"What started this thing?" Carl asked, breaking the silence. "If Segalini's been running dope from South America and Mexico like you said, why now? Why did he decide to take over the companies?"

"That's the part I can't answer yet. I found all of those manifests, some dated four years ago. He's been at it at least that long. The plants were imported from horticulturists in Mexico. Segalini would, at some point in the process, fill each plant pot with three packages of cocaine and ship them to the greenhouses in Virginia. He had all those people there to separate the stuff and repackage the plants for shipment to legitimate greenhouses and plant wholesalers all across the country. The packages of coke were shipped separately once they reached the transition site. The Virginia operation was a front, but a functional one. It looks like bags of cocaine were prepared for shipment to his crack houses where they were processed, some cut and sold as coke and some refined into crack. If you recall, when we hit the crack house in Jersey there were hundreds of bags of white powder in boxes. That was probably a new shipment just coming in. We hit them before they could process it."

"So he's making money on importing the plants and running cocaine in the process. Actually, the plant business is an expendable entity, but as a front it's invaluable. Okay, so where do Leeco and Boswell fit in?"

"Leeco and Boswell have ICC common-carrier routes to the exact locations where Segalini had his distribution points. Both companies run routes to the Mexican border. Boswell or Leeco could make direct delivery without offloading the plants. Boswell and Leeco also have the trailer rigs to maintain the temperature necessary to sustain the plants in unfavorable weather. Not all companies have that."

"How did you know that?"

"I worked on the docks. I also did a little homework while I was waiting for you to get to Dallas before they nabbed you."

"Couldn't any trucking company carry the goods for Segalini? Why did it have to be Leeco and Boswell?"

"Like I said, they have the routes. I also think Segalini's source at Leeco had a lot to do with it."

"Like who?"

"Think about it. It would have to be someone who could handle the numerous shipping manifests and have control of designating the routing."

"Who is that?"

"There are only three people at Leeco who have that authority. My dad, Logan Duggar, and Jill Lanier. Any one of them could assign a route or make a transfer to another carrier, namely Boswell."

"Shit, man, you think Jill's dirty?"

"I don't know. It wasn't Dad because Segalini wouldn't need to buy something he already had control of."

"So that leaves Duggar and Jill. Shit. Who do you think it is?"

"I'm not sure; all of the manifests were signed by Jill Lanier or Logan Duggar."

"Damn, man, I was beginning to think she was in love with you or something."

"She was . . . once."

"You drop her?"

"I guess you could say that. I joined the army."

"Yeah, you dropped her. Maybe she's just gettin' even."

"Could be." Marc Lee focused his attention on the highway again.

"Yeah, could be. Maybe they turned her."

"Hatred is a powerful motivator," Marc said.

"So's money."

"I won't argue that." Marc stopped the rig at a traffic light.

"What about Logan Duggar? How does he stack up?"

"My dad hired him when the company was very young. They built it together. Logan always made a comfortable living and Dad took care of him. Dad trusted him all these years. I can't see Logan doing that unless there is something we don't know."

"Maybe he wanted it all. What's your gut tellin' you? Is Jill layin' for your ass or is Logan Duggar hiding something?"

"I don't know yet, but I will soon."

The light turned green and Marc Lee started the big rig moving, changing gears and continually watching his mirrors. "Let's find a place to drop the rig and get the Ram ready," Marc said.

"I'm with you. The sooner we get this over, the better. It's a long way to Dallas. I'd like to be there for Christmas, for whatever good it would do."

"After all this, Christmas won't have quite the same feeling. You can relate to that, can't you?"

"Yeah, I can. This was supposed to be a break from the pressure. We haven't done something right." Carl Browne laughed. His ribs sent a searing pain through him and he stopped abruptly.

"I guess. There's a shopping mall ahead. If we can get through there for all the cars, we'll drop the rig."

"I'm ready. Yeah, brother, look at it on the bright side. At least the old man hasn't called."

"You're right, but I'll bet he's mad as hell by now. You can bet we're gonna hear about all this. The good general isn't going to be a happy man. You know how he is."

"Do I ever."

"And you know if the general is pissed, the big boss will be furious."

"He does have a tendency to get a little upset when there are no TV cameras around."

"Think positive. Something good may come of all this yet," Marc said as he drove the overroad rig into a giant shopping center parking lot.

Raffaello Segalini had not slept during the night. He was extremely disturbed over the conversation with Marzio Cavallo. It was beyond his comprehension that the council would meet without him. They had left him vulnerable and he wasn't taking any chances. He had instructed Anthony Johnson to secure additional men at whatever the cost, as long as their acquisition was expedient.

Anthony had complied and brought in every street hood who was indebted to them.

Raffaello had stood by the double French doors of his library overlooking Long Island Sound and watched the sun creep from the rolling waves. A housekeeper had served his breakfast, but he had no appetite.

He was standing by the French doors again, absorbing the view. The snow spanned to the water's edge and the waves visibly smoothed as they churned into the Connecticut shoreline across the Sound. He heard the door open behind him and he turned around.

"Boss, we got everything secure," Anthony Johnson said as he entered the library.

"Thank you, Anthony," Segalini said, his voice low.

"The pilot has been working on the chopper all day. He says everything is repaired now. Are you sure you want to stay here?"

"Yes, Anthony, I'm sure. I wouldn't miss this for the world."

"What about the coke we lost in Virginia? You want me to send some people in there to get whatever is left?"

"No, it's too risky. The place is swarming with police and who knows what else by now."

"Okay, whatever you say. When's the next shipment due in?"

"Next Tuesday."

"Where is it going?"

"I don't know yet. We have time to worry about that as soon as this matter is resolved."

"I see."

"How many people do we have armed?"

"About a hundred."

"Where did you get them . . . no, never mind, I don't want to know."

"Just as well."

"Get the servants out of here within the next hour. Be sure they have prepared enough food to last for a day or two as I requested. They have no part in this."

"Okay. Anything else?"

"Not at the moment. Thank you, Anthony."

Anthony left the room and Raffaello Segalini walked to his desk and sat in the highback chair. He opened a desk drawer and removed a Colt Pony 9mm automatic. He pulled the slide back and let it go. A round slid into the chamber. He clicked the safety on and placed the little gun in his coat pocket.

He rose from the chair and walked to the French doors. He stared out at the Sound and focused on his neighbor's yacht running along the shoreline about a half mile out. He thought it was a hell of a day to be out on the water. His thoughts wandered away. He thought of what the two commando truckers had done to his men in Dallas—to his only son, Bruno. His son, now incapacitated, confined to a wheelchair and struggling to stay alive. He had always planned to leave the business to him—groomed him for it. Bruno had proven his ability to handle problems and run the operation. And now his son was a cripple, mangled by some Texas truck driver and thrown into the darkened depths of depression because of his injuries. Bruno would never walk again. When Marc Lee and Carl Browne had severed his Achilles tendon with bolt cutters, they had also severed his link to voluntary mobility.

And for that, Raffaello Segalini had ordered the Lee family home destroyed, killing, quite by accident, Marc Lee's mother and uncle. And that, Segalini thought, is what had started this war. But now he wasn't finished. He wanted Leeco and he wanted the two men who had forever disabled his son. For Raffaello Segalini, it had long ago quit being business. . . . It was personal.

CHAPTER FOURTEEN

Marc Lee and Carl Browne had taken most of the afternoon to survey the Segalini estate. They had left the Dodge Ram 4 × 4 near the beach and had acquisitioned a boat a few miles from Segalini's compound. They had stowed their gear below deck and had taken the boat out into Long Island Sound. The water had been harsh, whitecapping. They had remained far away from the compound, a half-mile from the shoreline, to avoid unnecessary attention should Segalini have guards posted around the waterfront. They had anchored and were surveying the estate through Marc Lee's binoculars.

"Well, I'll be damned," Carl Browne said as he scanned the upper floor windows of the main residence. "There's our boy standing in front of a door in plain view."

"You're kiddin'. Let me see." Marc Lee took the binoculars and focused on a second-floor veranda with double doors. Raffaello Segalini was unsuspectingly standing at the doors, looking calmly into the rolling waters of the Sound. "He's either brave or crazy," Marc commented as he looked through the powerful rubber-armored binoculars and saw his enemy's face for the first time. "His being there tells me he isn't expecting us to come from the water."

"It's a damn shame we don't have the .50 caliber Long Range Rifle System. We could take that bastard out from here and save a lot of energy." Carl Browne was speaking of the new American Military Arms Corporation .50 caliber antiterrorist sensation that he and Marc Lee had insisted on for Delta Force use. It was a single-shot sniper rifle that was deadly accurate at over two thousand yards and could still deliver over one thousand foot-pounds of energy at that range. Hitting Segalini from the yacht with the LRRS would have been so easy.

Satisfied they had recorded a sufficient mental picture of their target, they took the boat to a long wooden pier jutting from the North Shore into the Long Island Sound. It was about a mile east of Segalini's estate. They moored there and waited for their natural habitat—darkness.

The estate had appeared affluent and secure, from Lee and Browne's observation point in the Sound. The main residence was a white brick Georgian-style house, situated on what Marc Lee estimated to be five or six acres. The main residence was two-story, the roof heavily tiled in hand-hewn and meticulously laid slate. The back of the residence faced north with a view of Long Island Sound and the Connecticut shoreline. The house was a hundred yards from the waterfront and secluded by towering sycamore and beech trees. If it had been summer, the house would have been hidden by leaves. The backyard covered almost three acres. The main residence was almost three hundred feet long. It looked more like a country clubhouse than a private residence. The lawn was mostly level, rising in the vicinity of a triangular flag near the western end of the estate, which Marc Lee suspected was a small golf course. A huge, in-ground, kidney-shaped swimming pool, aquatic blue against the snow-covered ground, was a hundred feet from the main residence toward the Sound. A small building, probably a pool house, sat just inside the tree line southwest of the pool. Further west from the pool, a high green fence rose from the snow, forming a rectangular enclosure for tennis courts.

The assault wouldn't be easy, but it could be done. Segalini's helicopter sat on the lawn, halfway between the main residence and the swimming pool. From the pier, Marc Lee and Carl Browne could see Segalini's long driveway. It came from the main road, weaved through the sycamores and beech trees, and ended in a circle directly in front of the entrance doors to the main residence. Another house, this one much smaller, sat nestled in the cover of the trees. It was also white brick, but only one story. It was the guest quarters.

The front of the estate was protected by a high brick wall running from the water's edge at the east side of the estate to the water's edge on the northwest corner. The area of private shoreline fronting Long Island was unprotected by anything but the cold ocean waters.

The formal address of the residence was Kings Point, New York. Indeed, the king of cocaine lived there—but he wouldn't be *living* there for long.

Marc Lee and Carl Browne spent the remainder of the afternoon inspecting and cleaning their weapons. They thoroughly checked each for function, obstructions, and serviceability. They opened a can of Military Ball 5.56mm ammo taken from the transition site in Virginia and reloaded each thirty-round magazine for the M-16's. Marc secured twenty-four M-79 incendiary fragmentation grenades in his bulging nylon musette bag. He had spare magazines for the M-16's, the Beretta 92-F, and the Desert Eagle .357 automatic.

Carl had his M-16, the Beretta 92-F, the Uzi, and the Model 19 Smith & Wesson he had retrieved from the dead hoodlum in the cave. He had his own coat and gloves, and had left the ones he had confiscated lying in the flaming ruins of the transition site. He carefully tucked the speed loaders for the .357 into his right coat pocket.

Surveillance from the Sound had revealed men lined behind the front wall, spaced about a hundred feet apart. There had been men moving on the flat top of a cabana at the rear of the main residence. They had seen men at every window at the back of the house. Judging from their offshore recon, there were more than fifty men armed and stationed around the estate. The Delta Warriors suspected more men were stationed where they couldn't be seen. They had counted only six men covering the shoreline.

Marc Lee looked at the face of his luminous watch and then glanced toward the western sky. It would be dark soon. "I figure another hour. They'll expect us to hit later. Might give us a little edge. What do you think?"

"Sounds reasonable."

Marc looked at Carl as the man finished preparing his weapons. "Just like we did it in Grenada?"

"It worked there. No reason why it won't work here," Carl said.

———

Clear liquid dripped from an inverted 500mm glass bottle attached to a stainless steel tubular rod and holder. The thin rod stood on a wheeled roller base sitting on the floor beside the therapeutic hospital-type bed. A clear plastic tube ran from the neck of the bottle at the drip adjustment valve and delivered glucose into Marcus Lee's left arm.

Numerous wires and attachments covered Marcus's chest beneath a hospital gown and ran to the inputs of a CRT cardiac monitor. A steady audible beep sounded in rhythm with his heartbeat. A single pale green plastic tube fed to his face and split into a pair of pale green nozzles just below his chin. The green tubing terminated in Marcus Lee's nostrils, giving him oxygen.

A nurse, dressed in white slacks and white pants sat beside his bed reading a romance novel. Another nurse, similarly dressed, sat across the small room and watched a television soap opera on a small color TV. The room was painted bright white. There were no windows and only one door for entry and exit. A restroom adjoined the room, separated by a single door.

Outside the room where Marcus Lee lay in a coma, there were four men. The room was littered with empty soft drink containers and several overflowing ashtrays. One man sat in a reclining chair digesting the latest issue of *Playboy,* while the other three were engrossed in a television movie.

A dining room and kitchen, off the main room where the men were sitting, formed an L-shaped large room. The kitchen was well stocked with an assortment of junk food and unopened soft drinks.

A fourth room, this one off of the main living room as well, contained three beds and another bathroom. At the moment, no one was in any of the beds.

The three men continued to watch the movie and the fourth remained engrossed in the girlie magazine. Two of the men were smoking cigarettes while the other two ate potato chips and onion dip. The living room was smoky, despite an air conditioner running steadily.

The apartment that held Marcus Lee was in the basement of a twenty-story downtown Dallas office building. The apartment was the only thing in the basement besides utility connections, a boiler, and several maintenance storage rooms. Entry into the basement section could be achieved only after passing through a series of five locked steel doors, each wired into a central alarm system terminating in the apartment.

There were six riot shotguns and four automatic assault rifles strategically placed around the main living room. Each man and nurse wore a handgun.

The man with the magazine got up from his chair and opened the door to Marcus Lee's room. "How's he doing?" he asked the nurses.

"Nothing's changed. This man has the vital signs of a nineteen-year-old. If you looked at him closely, you'd think he was just sleeping."

"Yeah, too bad. Call one of us if there is any change."

"We will."

"We still have plenty of drinks and chips out here if you care for some."

"No. Thanks, anyway. That stuff is bad for you. I'm an active young woman. I can't afford all the excess baggage."

"Have it your way. How about you?" The man asked, looking at the nurse who read the novel.

"I'm like Lena, I can't afford it either. Maybe later."

"All right, see you in a while." The man closed the door, shutting out the smoke that had started to seep into the treatment room from the living room.

"How's he doing?" one of the men absorbed in the movie asked.

"He's fine. Listen, I think I'm going to get some shut-eye before the boss comes by tonight. Wake me if you need anything. And remember, stay alert."

"You got it. Marcus is safe with us," the man replied. "This movie is not so hot, anyway. I think I'll read your *Playboy*."

"Have at it," the man said and tossed the magazine.

The man left the living room and walked into the bedroom. He removed his Model 459 Smith & Wesson 9mm automatic and placed it on a small table by the bed. He kicked his shoes off and unbuttoned his shirt. He laid down on the bed and tried to get comfortable.

Suddenly the man sat up. He started mumbling as he reached into the hip pocket of his jeans. "Damn badge— always hurts my ass." He placed the Dallas Police Department badge with its leather holder on the table beside the Smith & Wesson.

Marc Lee unholstered the Beretta 92-F. He pulled the slide back and released it. It slammed closed under the pressure of the recoil spring, then Marc stripped the top round from the magazine, and forced it into the chamber. He lowered the hammer gently, clicked the thumb safety on, and reholstered the weapon. He did the same with the Desert Eagle .357 automatic. He examined the edge on the long-blade Parker-Imai commando knife. It wasn't perfect, but it would do. He looked to Carl Browne as they both completed the weapons check. "You ready?"

"Whenever you are," Browne said as he closed the cylinder on the Model 19 .357 Combat Magnum.

"Let's do it," Marc said as he started the engine on the yacht. He steered the boat through the choppy water until they had almost reached the shore at the end of the pier. Lee steadied the boat, not wanting to hit the pier and cause unnecessary noise. He stopped and Carl Browne tied the boat to a wooden support pole on the long structure.

Marc Lee was out of the boat in seconds and onto the pier. Carl Browne handed him his musette bag and binoculars. The westerly wind had picked up and windchill was in the teens. Marc zipped his coveralls, stretched his fingers inside the Gore-Tex gloves, and pulled a black stocking cap over his ears. "I know this isn't your war. I can still go it alone if you'd rather wait it out. It's possible we won't come out of there. He's got a lot of shooters laying for us."

Carl laughed. "You're half right. He does have a lot of shooters waitin', but it *is* my war. I owe the bastard for my time on his stainless steel table. Let's go kick some ass!"

"See you there," Marc said. He ran the last few feet of pier and disappeared into the Long Island darkness. He heard the engine rev on the boat as he disappeared into the trees along the shore. He didn't look back as the engine faded into the choppy water and blackness, its sound smothered by the waves slapping ashore.

Marc made his way through the trees and onto the edge of Segalini's grounds. He moved slowly, running a few steps and crouching behind the cover of a tree.

He listened.

The sound of the yacht had faded completely. He worked further along the shoreline, weaving between trees and small shrubs. Five or six inches of snow covered the ground. It helped make his movement even more silent, more deadly.

Marc closed the distance to the estate. He stopped and crouched beside a huge beech tree, scanning the grounds as far as he could see. He searched for anything that shouldn't be there, any dark object that moved, however slightly.

He saw a movement thirty yards in front of him at the edge of the trees. He looked closer, the object now silhouetted against the snow and the ambient light from the main residence. It was a man. Marc remained motionless, his eyes focused on the area of the movement.

Marc watched the man for thirty or forty seconds, then moved silently toward him. He could see smoke trailing on the wind and whispering skyward into the darkness. The man was smoking a cigarette. He drew on the cigarette and then lazily dropped his left hand to his side. The red tip of the cigarette glowed like a beacon in the night, a fatal homing device.

Marc focused on the cigarette and his body tensed as he moved closer. The man stood against a giant sycamore, his back pressed against it, one leg bent at the knee and resting on the tree trunk. Marc could see an M-16 assault rifle in the man's right hand. He held it by the pistol grip, the muzzle harmlessly aimed into the snowy sand.

Marc paused less than forty-five feet from the man, scanning the remainder of the wooded area and shoreline. Waves crashed into the shore in steady rhythmic claps, driven harshly ashore by the gusting wind.

There was no sign of another sentry. The man was alone on the eastern shore of the estate.

Marc started his move. He slipped the Parker-Imai from its sheath and gripped it firmly in his right hand. He let the silenced Uzi drop to his side on the nylon sling. Marc stayed in a low crouch. He worked silently through the snow, moving from tree to tree as he narrowed the distance between him and his intended victim. It was less than twenty feet now. The man was undistracted, still casually smoking the cigarette.

There were only ten feet separating the men now. "Smoking's hazardous for your health, dipshit," he said, and he was running, closing the distance silently. Two more steps, one . . . Marc Lee's right arms wrapped around the man's mouth and face, pulling him from his perch. Marc's right knee jabbed into the man's back near the kidneys. The man stumbled, trying to regain his balance. Marc jerked at the man's neck, pulling it hard left. Something snapped with a loud, crunching pop. Marc Lee finished the man by running the Parker-Imai in a sweeping arc from the left side of his neck to the right, severing the aorta and esophagus. The cigarette and the M-16 fell noiselessly from the man's grip into the snow as the body crumbled to the ground.

Marc wiped the blade clean on the man's pants and left the body where it fell. He resheathed the huge knife and gripped the Uzi with his right hand as he moved closer to the brick security wall and the main residence. He could hear voices, the words indistinguishable over the wind and clapping waves. He kept moving, his senses on full alert and his instincts in total control of his functions.

The brick security wall was high, but it didn't go into the water's edge. There was an opening of perhaps three feet between the end of the wall and the water. Marc looked at it carefully, knowing there was surely a guard on the other side. He worked his way eastward again, toward the water of Long Island Sound. He reached the wall and fanned his body out against it as he listened for the location of the guard.

The sound of the waves as they collided with the shore dampened any strategically usable sound. If the guard was there, Marc Lee couldn't hear him.

Marc moved the safety off on the silenced Uzi subma-chine gun. He clicked the selector to full-auto. He worked up to the end of the wall, the distance between him and whatever waited on the other side less than three feet. He waited on the rhythm of the waves, pacing them as they crushed into the sandy shore. His mental timing registered the pattern. He waited for the last wave to slap the beach and start out into the ocean again. He took a deep breath and counted . . . one . . . two . . . three . . . four . . . *now!* He spun around the end of the wall, the Uzi at his right hip and his gloved finger curved around the trigger. Powdery snow flew in his wake as his feet covered the ground near the water. He fell into a low crouch, his eyes seeking a target.

A lone gunner sat against the wall with his knees up and feet on the ground. An assault rifle was between his legs, the muzzle pointing skyward. The man saw Marc as he rounded the end of the wall. He tried to react, to bring the assault rifle to a point of aim and scramble to his feet in one motion.

He was too late. Marc's finger was already hugging the

Uzi's trigger. Streaks of fire belched into the night like rapid bursts of close lightning, driving scorching lead into the man with deadly silence. The body shook visibly from the impact of each 9mm death missile. The man quivered, jerked, and then spread flat upon the ground as the final round disintegrated his larynx.

Lee moved to the man quickly, kicked his weapon from sight, and surveyed the grounds for another of Segalini's gunners. He saw none, but he knew they were there—somewhere.

Marc was running again, the lights from the main residence more prominent and lighting the way into the killing ground. He rounded a clump of hedges. A man appeared out of nowhere and stepped into his path. In his right hand was a revolver. Marc Lee dove into the snow as the man ducked to fire. Marc rolled right, spun a full 360 degrees in the snow, and his gloved finger found the Uzi's trigger. He jerked rather than squeezed, unleashing a solid full-auto burst. The man's body stopped all forward motion and vibrated under the impact of the 9mm bullets. The body seemed suspended in midair for an instant and then toppled backwards into the snow.

Marc was up quickly, snow falling from his Gore-Tex coveralls and the assault rifles slung across his back. He kicked the revolver the dead man had dropped and the weapon disappeared beneath the snow. He worked his way closer to the small guest house. The high brick wall was behind him; the armed goons he had seen from the boat were also at his back. He crouched beside a giant beech tree thirty yards from the small white brick house. Lee took three incendiary fragmentation grenades from his musette bag and stuck them into his belt. He squatted down in the snow, dropped the Uzi to his side on the sling, and pulled the M-16/M-79 from his right shoulder. He took a frag grenade from his belt and placed it in the launch tube below the rifle barrel of the assault weapon. Then he clicked the safety off and took aim across the weapon's carrying handle sights. His right index finger curved around the trigger and he squeezed gently. The rifle recoiled into his shoulder as the grenade left the bore. There was a soft *whoosh* and the tinkling of breaking glass, followed instantly by a bright flash and a loud explosion. The guest house erupted into flames, a large bay window in the front disappearing and scattering across the snow in shards of flying glass.

Marc reloaded the M-79 and touched off another grenade into a window at the opposite end of the guest house. There was another flash and fire flew from the window as a section of the wall cracked and collapsed to the ground.

He could hear the sounds of men screaming, running in panic, searching for the source of the incoming explosions.

Marc loaded the third round, aimed, and sent it flying through the front door. The door disappeared amid flames and flying debris.

Marc was up and running again. He crouched low behind the hedgerow fifty feet from the white brick house. Men ran into the yard, coughing and screaming, trying to ready their weapons. Marc steadied the M-16 and followed each panic-stricken man as he exited the burning house. He counted eighteen men. They were everywhere, looking, turning, spinning, moving around the lawn, talking and shouting in total disarray.

Marc slid the second M-16 from his shoulder, clicked the selector to full-auto, and flipped off the safety. He held both auto assault rifles by the pistol grips, parallel to the ground, the synthetic stocks tucked close to his sides and held firmly in place by his elbows. The index finger of each hand curved around a trigger, waiting for the moment to squeeze.

The Delta Warrior held his breath, his eyes locked on the men moving in the yard. He remained motionless beside the tree, his TreBark camo clothing blending with the beech tree's rough surface. He was poised, ready to react and send hellfire flying toward the frantic street punks.

Lee held his fire until the men were grouped together and silhouetted against the burning structure.

The men moved in absolute confusion. Lee heard more

voices—more men. This time they were behind him, coming from the front of the estate—from the fence.

He opened fire.

The M-16's rattled at full bore and sent hot .223 lead streaking through the night. Men were falling, screams of terror breaking over the sound of the gunfire.

Auto fire started from the men as bodies flopped to the snow, cut down eternally before most could react. Their shots went wild. Marc held the M-16's tightly against his side, fire from the flash suppressors lighting the night like a blowtorch, scorching his adversaries.

There was gunfire from behind him now. He was caught in the middle, the street hoods still not sure where the initial shots were coming from.

Lee saw a man running toward him, his auto gun blazing in the darkness. Marc spun the M-16 in his left hand at the man, unleashed a burst, and fired out the magazine. The man crumpled to the ground as the tiny bullets perforated his body.

The second M-16, the one in his right hand, fired out. Two men were coming, running from the group with auto guns spitting death. The bullets ripped a path to Marc Lee in the snow. He rolled right, tucking in the snow as the bullets dug deep burrows in the ground where he had been crouched. Marc dropped the M-16's on their slings and drew the Desert Eagle .357 Magnum automatic. He thumbed the safety down and worked the trigger. The big auto pistol roared and recoiled in his hand. He did a double-tap, followed immediately by another, the auto gun rocking and returning to point of aim under the recoil. The two men fell.

Marc fired the Desert Eagle into the men in the yard who still hadn't found cover. He slipped the Desert Eagle into his waistband, the slide locked back, and grabbed the M-16's. He buttoned down the empty magazine from first one, then the other. He grabbed fresh sticks from his nylon musette bag and slapped them into the wells of the auto rifles. He worked one bolt back, then the other, and crammed a round into each chamber. He brought the weapons on line and the auto guns chattered their death chant.

There was more gunfire, this time from the back of the main residence. Lee was up in a run, zigzagging through the snow from one big tree to another. Bullets pelted the trees where he stood, absorbed harmlessly by the hardwood.

He kept running, the night alive with deadly gunfire.

Carl Browne had landed. The explosion of the first frag grenade had been his cue to move in. He had opened the yacht to full throttle and headed straight into the sandy beach behind the estate. The yacht had run aground with a groaning thud. Even before it stopped, Browne was out, running across the lawn.

Five men came at him from the beach perimeter.

Browne fell on line with the M-16's at his side. Gunfire rained into the men from both of Browne's hands, empty brass hissing as it hit the cold snow. The men fell into the snow along the beach, rolled face-first into the water, and disappeared into the choppy blackness.

Browne kept charging across the back lawn. He could hear Lee's fire from the front. The Desert Eagle stood out from the rapid-firing auto guns, the roar deeper and more resonant.

Four men atop the cabana in the rear of the house opened up at Carl Browne. Their shots missed and hammered harmlessly into the snow. Browne spun the auto rifles toward the men, hip-shooting as he ran a bob-and-weave pattern across the lawn. He saw two men fall and heard their final screams as death took them on its wings and flung them from the rooftop.

A massive explosion, followed by intense light, rocked the ground. Marc Lee had driven a frag grenade into the main residence. The grenade entered a front window and the concussion sent glass shrapnel sailing across the back lawn.

Carl Browne hit the snow spread-eagle, his hands still holding the M-16's and covering his head.

The rain of glass stopped and Browne was up again,

firing into the windows of the main residence. Flames licked from the lower floor windows as another grenade erupted.

Browne looked to his right, along the swimming pool. Men were coming at him, their guns chanting death. Browne spun and crouched, firing out the M-16's. Bullets hit three of the men, two of them plunging sideways into the aqua blue swimming pool. The lighted blue pool became clouded with misty patterns of red fanning out like long tentacles.

Four more men came at Carl Browne. There was no time to reload. Browne let the M-16's fall to his side on the slings. He was out in a smooth motion with the Beretta 92-F. He doubled-actioned the first round into the face of the man nearest him. The man fell, his face smeared in blood and torn tissue.

Three men kept charging, undaunted by their fallen contemporaries. Browne opened up with the Beretta. He dumped fifteen rounds as fast as he could squeeze the trigger. The men fell like dominos.

The slide locked back on the Beretta and Browne shoved it into his waistband.

He was running again, past the helicopter and toward a service entrance at the rear of the house. He jumped toward a door as bullets rattled the brick wall beside him. Another man appeared—bigger than Carl Browne—firing an automatic pistol. Browne reached for the Smith & Wesson. The bore was parallel to the ground as he double-actioned the weapon twice. The magnum rounds struck the man in the chest and he toppled backwards. Browne started to turn when the man popped off a round from his dying hand. Carl double-tapped again and the man was finished.

Browne hit the door with a front snap kick just as another grenade exploded somewhere in the upstairs of the house. The door swung open, jarred from its hinges. Carl Browne was in.

He stopped just inside the cover of the small mud room to reload. He buttoned down the magazines from the empty M-16's and crammed new ones in the wells. He worked the bolts and readied the auto guns. He swung the cylinder open on the Smith & Wesson Model 19 and ejected the empties. A swift reach into his coat pocket produced an HKS speedloader. He stuck the rounds into the cylinder, twisted the button, and slammed the cylinder closed. He was reaching for the empty Beretta when a gunner appeared across the small room through another door. The man fired, but his shots missed. Browne dropped the 92-F to the floor and grabbed the pistol grip of the M-16 on his right side. He rolled to the floor as more shots missed him. Then he spun out of the roll, the M-16 spitting death. The gunner vibrated in sync with the fire belching from the assault rifle as he crumpled and fell.

Browne retrieved the Beretta and put a fresh stick up the butt, thumbed the slide stop down, and lowered the hammer. He placed the 9mm automatic in his waistband on his left side.

Carl Browne broke through a sunken living room and across the front of the house. Fires were raging, consuming the dwelling. Thick black smoke billowed from the burning contents. He reached the front door just as Marc Lee burst through.

They gave each other the thumbs-up sign and started searching the house. A winding staircase spiraled up to the second floor. The entry foyer was open, spanning two full stories of the residence and creating a giant open area immediately surrounding the front door.

Carl Browne went left, across the foyer and into the remaining portion of the first floor. Marc Lee took the steps.

Lee reached the top without opposition, his auto rifles ready. He turned down a long corridor to his right when the front door opened behind him. A man with a shotgun stepped in. Lee spun around and shot the man with a three-round burst to the head before he could react. The man catapulted back out the door, dead.

Lee continued down the hallway, searching and kicking doors as he went. Still no gunfire, no opposition. Segalini had been on the east end of the house at the rear. Marc tried to visualize the room from the inside by picturing its location on the exterior of the house.

His mental visualization told him it would be three doors further on his left. He moved carefully as gunfire still slammed into the house from the outside. Flames licked the interior, breaking through to the attic now. Smoke billowed in churning cyclones as the fire ignited by the incendiary grenades raged and consumed Raffaello Segalini's refuge.

Marc heard gunfire from the first floor. Long, full-auto bursts resonated through the smoky house. Then three roaring booms from Carl's .357 magnum.

Marc Lee crouched low to breathe, almost in a duck walk. He reached another door, the smoke thicker now, flames lapping from the walls and making breathing difficult. He listened for a second, then stood erect and hit the door with a snap kick. The door flew open as Marc rolled to the floor.

A flash, partially obscured by the smoke, was followed instantly by a booming crash as a man fired a shotgun toward the door. The pellets missed and slammed into the wall above Marc Lee's head.

Marc sprayed the room with auto fire, cleansing it of scum. He heard the hostile weapon hit the floor, followed by a loud thud when the gunner entered eternity.

He kept moving, sure the auto spray had swept the room clean. He reached the second door, this one on his right, at the front of the house. He kicked the door in. Flames belched into his face, singeing his hair. He slammed it closed again. If anyone was in there, he would let them burn.

According to Marc's evaluation of the residence, the next door should be the one leading to the veranda where they had seen Segalini. Marc readied a kick, struck, then rolled inside. As he came out of the roll, he was at the feet of a man standing at least six-eight. Marc tried to fire, but a huge foot snapped the M-16 from his hands, breaking the sling. Marc rolled again, trying to evade the man. He lost the Uzi in the roll when it fell from his shoulders. He reached for the Beretta, but a huge fist landed against his jaw. The impact burned and jolted his brain. Marc lost his footing and fell. The man kicked again, a big foot landing in Marc's ribs. Again there was intense burning pain. Marc gasped as smoke filled the room and complicated his efforts to breathe. He struggled for air and another fist landed against his head. Little twinkling lights stirred around the room as Marc fought to save his consciousness. The man was on him, thrashing and pounding. Marc tasted blood, his own, dripping from his mouth and the side of his head. The big man wouldn't retreat as he brutally attacked Marc's body. Each new motion from the man brought Marc greater pain. His brain was losing light, and all his control of balance was gone.

The Desert Eagle—Marc tried to find the Desert Eagle .357 auto. His hands fumbled, beating at the side of his pants, but it was gone.

Marc tried to kick the man, but his legs were rubbery. His arms wouldn't move his fists and they sank to his sides—first his left, then his right.

He found the Parker-Imai.

Marc struggled to free the knife. It cleared the sheath with the big man still throwing punches like a savage beast. The blade was in position. Marc made a final, all-out thrust.

The blade ripped through flesh. Blood dripped onto Marc as someone else in the room screamed, "Kill the son of a bitch, Anthony! Kill him, Anthony! *Kill him!*"

Marc twisted the blade with the last energy remaining in his body. He shoved the dead man from atop him and stumbled to his feet.

Raffaello Segalini sat calmly at his desk, dressed in an expensive dinner jacket, and said, "You didn't kill him, Anthony? You failed me."

CHAPTER FIFTEEN

Marc Lee stared hellfire at the man.

Segalini was solemn. "So you're Marc Lee. I knew you'd come, Mr. Lee. Tell me something, are you human? Really?"

Marc stood there, the bloody Parker-Imai dangled in his right hand. "Why, Segalini? Why did it have to be Leeco? Why not any of a dozen others? Why my father's company?"

"You don't understand, Mr. Lee—business. Something a Texas redneck would know nothing about."

"Why did you kill my mother, you bastard?" Lee's lips pursed and his face filled with anger.

"It was an accident. She was supposed to be at the hospital. I only ordered your home demolished. Purely an accident."

"Why Leeco? Or do you want me to kill you now?"

"No harm, I suppose. I'm going to kill you anyway," Segalini said as he produced a small pistol from his pocket and pointed it at Marc Lee. "You lose, Mr. Lee. You don't have a gun."

"So kill me, then. My partner is downstairs; you'll never leave this place alive. Go ahead, kill me."

"To answer your question, Mr. Lee, Leeco was of strategic value and we already had someone inside. It was natural."

"Who do you have inside?"

"Sorry, Mr. Lee. You'll die and never know."

Marc Lee lunged when the man squinted his eyes against the smoke filling the room. The big Parker-Imai blade caught Segalini's gun arm, passed through flesh, and riveted into the desk top. The little handgun fell to the floor.

Segalini screamed. It was a long, crying scream of bitter agony blended with fulfilled fear.

Marc jumped back, found his Beretta, and retrieved the M-16/M-79. "No, asshole, you lose."

Segalini was still screaming, trying to pull the knife from the desk, trying to free his arm. His eyes were bulging. Blood poured from the severed arteries in his arm. He screamed louder, a long, tormented scream. Then he stopped, rage in his face. "Why did you cripple my son, you bastard?" he yelled as he still tried to free the knife.

"Your son?" Marc asked, not hiding his surprise. He kept his weapons aimed at Segalini.

"Yes, damn it. Bruno, my son. You crippled him. You son of a bitch, you crippled him!"

"We really didn't know, not that it would have mattered. You remember my note? I said the fifth one was for you. I'm gonna fill it now," Marc Lee said softly as he backed to the door. He reached down and picked up the Uzi and the Desert Eagle. Fire was raging in the hallway outside. Smoke was unbearable and breathing was extremely difficult. Marc loaded an incendiary grenade into the muzzle of the M-79 as he moved backwards. "Since you like to blow things up so much, I'm gonna give you one last fiery flash for your grand finale." Marc stepped into the hallway, the M-79 pointed straight at Segalini.

"Don't do this. Please, don't do this to me." Segalini was screaming, begging. He struggled bitterly with his good arm and hand to free the knife driven deeply into the mahogany desk top. "It was just business, I swear. Business."

"Have a good time in hell, scumbag." Marc Lee fingered the trigger and rolled into the hallway. A bright flash filled the smoky room for an instant. Segalini was still screaming, but the screams vanished amid a deafening explosion as the room disintegrated and turned into a hellish inferno.

Marc was up from the roll, running toward the entry

foyer. He hit the top of the stairs and bounded down in three or four leaps. Carl Browne was coming from a wing to Lee's left when he reached the bottom. The house was a raging torrent of fire now, blazing beyond any control.

"Let's tote it, brother. I got the chopper keys from the pilot," Browne said.

"Where's the pilot?" Marc asked.

"Crazy bastard pulled some damn little pistol on me, so I wasted him. I take it that big bang was in honor of Raffaello?"

"Yeah," Marc said.

"Where is he?" Carl asked.

"On his way to hell."

They started from the foyer toward the mud room in the back. Suddenly Carl stopped and swung his M-16 on line with a movement at the top of the stairs.

It was a man wearing a robe, seated in a wheelchair, overlooking the foyer. His hands lay atop a blanket folded in his lap. His head was slumped down as if he were tired or depressed.

Browne started to finish the man, whose true features were obscured by the intense smoke. He appeared as an illusion against a sea of fire. Flames licked the walls and floors beside him and the ceiling started to collapse all around him. But still he didn't move—he just looked at the two Delta Warriors with a vacant, defeated stare as the blazing appendages of death reached for him.

"Leave him," Marc said. "That's Bruno. He's Segalini's son. He's harmless like that."

"Well, what do you know about that," Carl said, more a statement than a question. "I never would have guessed it." And he dropped the muzzle of the M-16.

"Let him go like this," Marc said, motioning toward the fire. "It'll help him get ready for hell."

———

Marc Lee and Carl Browne had finished Segalini's estate with five incendiary grenades into the main residence. They had made their way to the chopper. Most of Segalini's hired guns had deserted. The others had died.

Marc had run a brief preflight inspection of the helicopter. It had been undamaged in the firefight. He had dropped Carl off at the Ram down the beach from Segalini's estate. Carl had agreed to run the rig back to Dallas. Marc had reviewed the navigational charts already in place in the cockpit and had flown directly to Dallas, except for two fuel stops. He had landed at a small airfield in Garland, Texas, a few miles from Dallas. He had immediately called Brittin Crain and the detective had agreed to meet him at the airport.

"Well, old boy, you've sure stirred up a lot of shit for yourself. Can't say I blame you, though. Now what's this you're tellin' me?" Crain asked as he drove the unmarked Dodge police car toward Dallas.

"All the manifests were signed by Jill Lanier or Logan Duggar. They dated back over four years. Somebody's dirty."

"You know, Marc, I've known you and Jill since we were all in high school together—when you two were lovers. It just doesn't add up. It isn't her style."

"It has to be her or Logan Duggar. They're the only two who can sign a manifest, except my father."

"You think maybe it's her way of gettin' back at you—that is, if it's her?"

"Hell, Brittin, I don't know why she would do something this radical. We parted as friends—at least I thought so."

"I say it's Logan Duggar."

"He's certainly had the opportunity, but what's his motivation?"

"I'm not sure. It could be anything. Anyone capable of involvement in this kind of melee doesn't need a lot of motivation. It could be something we'd consider insignificant, but he'd consider paramount. The human mind is unpredictable sometimes."

"How well I've learned that in dealing with terrorists."

Marc Lee and Brittin Crain were near Leeco Freight

Lines. "When we go in, we have to act like everything is okay," Marc said. "Don't act like we have any knowledge of anything out of place until I start talking, okay?"

"Boy, every time I get around you I end up breakin' all the rules. Just like when we played football."

"What are friends for?"

"Yeah, shit. I wonder that myself sometimes."

"You say my father's condition is unchanged?"

"Right."

"Has the medical staff offered anything new?"

"No. Since we took him from the hospital that night and left the drunk orderly, they've been with him around the clock. He looks like he's sleeping—I guess maybe he is."

"He'll come out of it," Marc said. "He's got to."

"He will. Believe me, he will. I think we did the right thing by taking him from the hospital. Leaving him unprotected was much too risky."

"Thanks. I thought someone might try to hit him after what they did to Mom."

"Yeah, I'm really sorry about that. Your mom was always like a mother to me, too. She was a friend."

They reached Leeco Freight Lines. Brittin Crain parked the police car and both men started into the building. As they reached Jill's office, she saw them and screamed. She ran to Marc Lee and wrapped her arms around him, squeezed him, and pressed her body against his. "Marc. Oh, Marc, I'm so glad you're okay. I was worried sick. I thought maybe you wouldn't come back—that maybe they'd killed you. Oh, Marc, I love you—I love you." She hugged him again, not wanting to turn him loose.

The final piece fell in place and then Marc Lee knew—New Jersey—the truckstop—the phone call.

Marc didn't know what to say. He kissed Jill Lanier and held her tightly. "You know I'm too mean to die," he said and smiled. "Where's Logan?"

"In his office, I guess. Why?" Jill was still holding his arm.

"Call him in here for me, will you? Oh—you remember Brittin Crain, don't you?"

"Of course. You're a policeman now, aren't you, Brittin?"

"Yes, I am, Jill. Nice to see you again. It's been awhile."

"I'll call Logan." She let go of Marc and went back to her desk, pressing a button on the intercom and asking Logan Duggar to come into the room.

Less than a minute passed and Logan Duggar entered the office. "Marc, thank goodness you're all right. Is it over?"

"Yes, Logan, almost."

"That means we can get back to business as usual, then?"

"I don't think business will ever be as usual again," Marc said.

"I don't know what you mean, Marc."

"I think you do, Logan. We have evidence that Segalini has had somebody on the inside running his dope shipments to the north for years. My money's on you, Logan," Marc said, and fire filled his eyes. "I knew a few pieces wouldn't fit. But then it hit me. You had the perfect cover—you were setting Jill up. You're the only one who has enough control inside Leeco to be able to pull something like this off for any length of time. No one would question you."

"Marc, you can't be serious, can you? Why me?"

"I had planned to let you answer that, Logan. Since you're playin' dumb, I'll do it for you. You, Jill, and my father are the only ones in this company who are authorized to make a manifest assignment. We found a four-year history of manifests in Virginia at a place called Vesuvius, your dope transition site. Does that mean anything to you?"

"No, I can't say it does," Duggar said.

"All of those manifests were signed by Jill or you. But then, you're the one who does the routing. So I started thinking, what does Leeco have in common with J. T. Boswell Trucking. Then it hit me—Logan Duggar—you worked there before you came with my father. It all came together when I walked in the door a few minutes ago. Is it making a little better sense now, Logan?" Marc asked.

Logan Duggar didn't answer.

Marc continued. "A few days ago in New Jersey, when our driver was killed, he told us he had just talked to the weekend dispatcher. That dispatcher was you, Logan. When our trucks were blowing up all over the country, you were the only person in this company who would have know where every rig was at any given time. And then Carl and me, when we were on the road—you knew which rig we were in, knew the probable routes we would have to take. It has to be you."

Duggar lunged for Jill Lanier. He grabbed her and his left arm flew around her neck. He applied pressure, almost choking her. A small pistol appeared in his right hand. "Get back, all of you. I'll kill her. I mean it. Get back. I'm leaving."

"I don't think so, Logan," Marc said, the Beretta at arm's length and the sights aligned directly between Logan Duggar's eyes.

"I'll kill her. Get out of my way."

"Why, Logan? Why, after all these years working side by side with my father?"

"Money, strictly money. Sure, I worked side by side with your father. He made all the money and I made a salary. I built this company just as much as he did and he never offered me a partnership."

"Why didn't you leave? No one forced you to stay."

"It's not that easy. I earned part of this business."

Jill Lanier was turning white, listless. Her eyes were huge and filled with fear. She didn't move—she couldn't.

"He took the financial risks, Logan. He paid you well. And my mother—you slimy bastard. You helped kill my mother."

"No, no . . . it wasn't supposed to be like that. It was meant to scare you. We weren't trying to kill her. It was an accident."

"Accident or not, she's still dead, Logan."

Brittin Crain was just standing there, feeling helpless.

"I started thinking about retirement. There was nothing there—no money, just a pension and Social Security.

Marcus had it all and I had nothing. I knew he'd retire before too many more years and probably sell the company. Then where would I be? You had no interest in the company, so I'd be out in the streets. I'm too old for that, Marc."

"How did the mob turn you?"

"Like I said, money. They paid me well to manipulate the manifests, assign the routing. I kept quiet and did what they wanted me to do."

"That's greed, Logan."

"Maybe so, but I don't see it that way. I wasn't going to be kicked out in the streets with nothing."

"So you ran dope and caused innocent people to die—all for money. I don't believe this. And my father trusted you." Marc stepped toward Duggar.

"Get away from me. Put that gun down. I swear I'll blow her brains out."

"Come on, Mr. Duggar, don't make it any worse. Give me the gun," Brittin Crain said as he motioned his hand toward the weapon at Jill Lanier's head.

"Do what he says, Logan. Don't make it any worse," Marc said, never taking his eyes off of Duggar across the Beretta's sights.

"That's close enough, I'll kill her."

"Give me the gun, Logan," Marc said and he moved closer.

"Get back and away from the door. I'm going out of here. Don't try to stop me or I really will blow her brains out." The man was sweating, streaks of perspiration running from his forehead. His voice was trembling and he was shaking.

"I'm sure you will, Logan. But we're not moving. You'll have to kill us, too."

"You mean you'd kill her rather than let me leave?"

"Oh, no, you got it all wrong, Logan. You see, you'll kill *her*—and then I'll kill *you*!" Marc said through clenched teeth. The Beretta never moved from its intended target.

Logan Duggar started to move. Jill Lanier's eyes rolled back into her head and she fainted. Her body weight was too much for Logan to handle with one hand. He lost his grip and Jill collapsed to the floor. Logan was wide open and Marc's Beretta pointed at his chest. He jerked the small pistol toward Marc Lee and fired a futile shot. His scream filled the room with his private agony.

Marc Lee squeezed the Beretta's trigger twice.

It was personal.

ABOUT THE AUTHOR

Bob Ham grew up in a rural environment in the Blue Ridge Mountains just outside of Roanoke, Virginia. Throughout his youth, he spent most of his leisure time outdoors learning about nature firsthand. In the time between high school and college, Bob worked for a national trucking firm. He attended college in Roanoke and later studied law.

Bob has an extensive background in law enforcement. His experience ranges from traffic patrol to detailed undercover operations involving narcotics, drugs, and firearms.

In the mid-seventies, Bob left the mountains of Virginia for Nashville, Tennessee. He gave up law enforcement for a career in the country music business. His diverse music business career is now in its second decade. He owns a record promotion and marketing firm that has continuously set industry track records since its inception in 1980.

Aside from his music and law enforcement interests, Bob is also an authority on firearms and radio communications. He is an avid hunter, fisherman, and sport shooter. He is currently a qualified Expert with both shotgun and submachine gun and a qualified Master with a pistol and revolver. He occasionally shoots competitively in regional law enforcement competitions as a member of the Williamson County Sheriff's Department combat pistol team.

Bob Ham is licensed as an Advanced Class amateur radio operator. In his spare time, he is active on the amateur radio bands and has made thousands of radio contacts throughout the world. His radio hobby also gives him the opportunity to experiment with various types of antennas and electronic devices including computers, repeaters, packet radio, and radioteletype.

The extensive "hands-on" knowledge Bob has accumulated in electronics, radio, firearms, law enforcement, outdoor survival, and the trucking industry blends together in his adventure books to keep the reader entertained.

Bob and his wife reside in Brentwood, Tennessee, with their two children.

ACTION ON EIGHTEEN WHEELS!

Here is a special preview
of Book #2 in the OVERLOAD series:
THE WRATH by Bob Ham

Look for OVERLOAD
wherever Bantam Books are sold.

CHAPTER ONE

Bruno Segalini sat in his wheelchair beside the hydraulic chair lift on the beige van. He surveyed the ruins of his father's estate in Kings Point on the North Shore of Long Island, New York.

The house was charred rubble—a grim reminder of The Night—the night he lost his father, their house, and their business at the hands of Marc Lee and Carl Browne. Lee and Browne had left him to die as fire raged all around him and consumed the house. He had miraculously escaped and suffered only bruises and minor cuts.

He looked down at his legs, hidden beneath a quilted blanket—they were useless appendages. Marc Lee and Carl Browne had scarred him forever—crippled him. His Achilles tendons had been cut—severed by bolt cutters when Lee and Browne had surprised him and three associates in the Dallas headquarters of Leeco Freight Lines. The only consolation Bruno Segalini felt was knowing his people had killed Marc Lee's mother and uncle. He had personally left Marcus Lee, Marc's father, lying unconscious in a pool of blood on his office floor. Marc Lee and Carl Browne had thwarted the mob's takeover efforts at Leeco Freight Lines. What followed had been a bloody and costly war— for both sides.

Now, Bruno Segalini intended to end the battle forever. When Marc Lee and Carl Browne were dead, he would fulfill the secret oath he had made to his father. He would continue the family business and keep the cocaine flowing.

A man approached him. He was a large man with a muscular physique. He was wearing a dark suit and dark sunglasses. His hair shone in the sunlight. It was Johnny "Ceps" Cressen, so named by his friends because of his massive biceps. He was Segalini's last "aide-de-camp," and it was with his help that Bruno was preparing the "final solution" for Lee and Browne. He stopped beside the wheelchair and crossed his arms. He looked at the ruins, then at Bruno, his solid face void of expression.

Bruno Segalini looked up at the man. "Is it all in place?" he asked.

"Yes sir, just as you requested. He was contacted last night and we have reached a mutual agreement. It seems he is just as anxious as you are," Ceps said.

"Good."

Ceps turned immediately and disappeared behind the van into the trees surrounding the estate.

A cool morning breeze blew across the waters of Long Island Sound. Misty ocean spray filled the air with the smell of salt. The cool air and the salt stung Bruno Segalini's nostrils. He looked back for one final moment at what had been his home—his father's home. He stared vacantly at the devastation as his mind replayed the memories. And from the ashes came the fire—and it filled his heart with wrath.

Mike Garland was twenty feet from the cab of his Leeco rig when he heard the rumble. It sounded like a swarm of bumblebees rhythmically vibrating a bass staccato. The truck driver turned, seeking the source of the sound, and faced the first glittering fingers of the morning sun.

When he saw it, his heart sank and his stomach heaved upward into his chest.

The big driver stood frozen, unsure how to react, afraid to overreact—yet more afraid to do nothing. His wavy brown hair almost rose from his head. Every muscle in his six-foot body tensed. All he could think of was his .38 revolver lying in the cassette tape console in the rig, useless. Reflexively, Mike Garland thought of the ongoing national debate about truckers carrying guns. Its proponents, and Mike was one of them, felt truckers should be armed to protect themselves, their rigs, and their cargoes from hijackers. And just now, Mike Garland *knew* that they were right.

The bumblebees were idle now. Mike made a fast mental count of them—thirty-two, give or take a couple because of his nerves. Suddenly, it was like Vietnam all over again—that helpless feeling knowing they had you, wondering what they were going to do, wondering, more importantly, what you shouldn't do. This was survival at the most basic level again and there had been no warning.

Garland scanned the parking lot for help, for anyone, but there was no one there—no one except the bikers.

It didn't take a genius to figure out what these people were. Their sheer number, their dress, and their rumbling Harleys meant only one thing—trouble. He saw a miniature skull and crossbones mounted on a handlebar, a swastika on another. Each bike had a chrome Maltese cross extending up from the rear of the seat, like the back of a chair. Three of the filthy bikers wore linked motorcycle chains for belts. He saw another with a North American Arms belt buckle and a .22 caliber derringer mounted in the middle of it. All the bikers looked alike. They were dirty with heavy beards. Their denim jeans were unwashed and faded. Each man wore a black leather jacket fully appointed with silvery chrome snaps, buttons, and brads. On the left front of each jacket in black-and-white gothic type was the word LOBO.

Mike Garland digested it all—LOBO—wolf. And that's that they looked like, a pack of hungry preying wolves, salivating beside a carcass they intended to devour.

Garland decided it wouldn't be his carcass they feasted upon. He turned and started to walk to the Freightliner. He was mentally pretending these filthy human beings weren't there. Screw the opponents of the debate—if he could only get to the .38.

"Hey, dad. Where you goin'? You unsociable or what?" It was the biker at the front of the human wolf pack, obviously the leader. The man sat astraddle a chrome-trimmed Harley-Davidson Low-Rider, with both feet on the pavement, balancing the bike. He was a huge man, over six-three. Garland guessed him to be about two hundred and twenty pounds. He wore dark green sunglasses and had wiry brown hair and a matted, gray-streaked brown beard. His body vibrated with the idling motorcycle; his arms were folded across his chest.

"You talkin' to me?" Garland asked, attempting to display confidence in his voice.

"Yeah, man, I'm talkin' to you," the leader biker said. "You see anybody else in this pickle park?"

There was a different roar now. It was laughter rippling through the pack of bikers.

"What can I do for you boys?" Garland asked, not really wanting an answer.

The lead biker started laughing. "Funnyman. Look, dudes, we got us a funnyman, a regular friggin' comedian. You don't understand, man. It ain't what you can do for us—it's what we're gonna do *to* you. We're gonna make an example out of you, man. We're gonna show your new boss, Marc Lee, what happens when you screw around with the wrong people. You know, like he's pissed off *the man*, can you dig?"

"I don't know what you're talkin' about. I just drive this truck and make my runs. I don't have anything to do with what the company does." Garland felt the gastric juices flowing, the adrenaline rush spreading throughout his body like a tidal wave. He had to make a move, but what? Take the point man first, he thought to himself, crush his esophagus and let him smother to death. Then, take the others as they come until there's no fight left.

"Well, since you're shark bait anyway, I'm going to explain it to you," the big lead biker's voice was radiating confidence. "Like your man, this Marc Lee dude, thinks he's some kind of supercommando, you see. Like he's screwed up my sources for lines, you dig? I mean, when you start messin' with my coke, man, you're messin' with my dough. And me and my people here, well, we dig our lines and we make a bunch of money sellin' to the street. So, anyway, this Marc Lee killed my snowman, Mr. Segalini. But, he messed up. He thought he had killed the old man's son, Bruno, too. But the kid came through and he hired us to take care of Marc Lee so we can get our sources back in the pipeline. I'm a commando too, you see. I want Marc Lee so I can kill him with my bare hands—just like what I did in Vietnam—soldier against soldier—purpose against purpose. Only I'm better than he is. I'm some kind of bad, you dig?" The man threw his hands into the air, hesitated, and let them drop to his sides as he laughed again.

Mike Garland remained frozen. Here he was, at a desolate rest area on an interstate highway in eastern South Carolina, surrounded by a drooling band of bloodthirsty bikers led by some sicko Vietnam vet whacked out on cocaine, and his gun was in the cab of his truck—twenty feet away.

The intensity of the rumble increased. The bikers started moving, circling him and taunting him. It was almost like the old Westerns he had watched as a kid when attacking Indians were stalking a wagon train. He suddenly felt as he thought an animal in the wild must feel when a pack of wolves surround it just before the kill.

But if he was their prey, they would have to take him. He started his mental timing. He watched his intended first victim as the bikers continued to circle him. He waited and then he lunged.

Gary Martin lifted the bottom edge of the corrugated cartons and slid the two-wheeled dolly's lip beneath them. He started moving the dolly backward out of the trailer in the direction of the Leeco Freight Lines loading dock. He was half-finished unloading the Consolidated Freight trailer. Dawn was starting to break across the eastern horizon of south Dallas. Martin wanted to have at least three-fourths of the freight unloaded and transferred by the time he finished his shift at seven o'clock. Although most of the boxes weren't large, they were unusually heavy. The entire shipment was from a New York importer consigned for transfer and distribution in south Texas. From what Gary Martin could tell by the package markings, the boxes contained electronic equipment.

The dolly was almost across the steel loading platform connecting the end of the trailer with the dock when, suddenly, the top box became extremely hot. Martin lost his grip on the load as he jerked his hand away from the heat. The box dislodged and fell to the platform. Martin stopped the dolly and started to reach for the carton, thinking the heat was only his imagination—boxes didn't just all of a sudden become hot. But then he jumped back and away from it. On impact with the dock, the carton had started smoking. Before Martin could get to a fire extinguisher, the box erupted in flames. He started running and screaming, "Fire! Fire! Fire at twenty-three. Somebody call the fire department."

Jim Howard was the midnight-shift dock foreman. The instant he heard Gary Martin's cry for help, he dialed the fire department and grabbed the nearest fire extinguisher. Howard ran toward port 23 in a full sprint, shouting orders to the other workers on the dock. "Harry, Jimbo, get every fire extinguisher you can find and break out the fire hoses. This son of a bitch is heading out of control. Hustle up!"

The dock workers didn't hesitate. They ran for port 23 like sailors manning battle stations. Smoke filled the transfer dock and the fire raged. Visibility diminished rapidly. Three men, one of them a driver who had been waiting in the lounge for his trailer to be unloaded, ran with fire extinguishers to dump them on the blazing carton. But by the time they reached port 23, all the cartons were ablaze.

The fire was burning white-hot with rancid white metallic smoke bellowing into the off-loading transfer area of Leeco Freight Lines. The heat from the burning cartons was so intense, the steel platform bridging the gap from the trailer to the dock at port 23 was already glowing red. The dolly Gary Martin had been using to move the freight was now only glowing twisted metal beneath a halo of fire.

In an instant, the entire west end of the dock was blazing out of control. It had taken less than thirty seconds for the fire to spread to the other cartons and to other freight loads in distribution or transfer trailers. Jim Howard knew the blaze would completely destroy the loading dock and warehousing area in another five minutes if it remained unchecked. "Jimbo, get the hose going. Hit it with everything you've got. Larry, get another hose over here. Start spraying the freight behind us. Soak everything before this mother becomes cinders."

"Right, boss," Larry Michaels said as he grabbed a reeled fire hose and opened the cock.

The smoke intensified and breathing was difficult. The workers, who had stopped doing everything else to fight the fire, were now fighting for air—for life.

"Some of you men get the vacant ports open. Get any drivers in the lounge to pull their rigs away from the dock. If the keys are in any other rigs, get them the hell out of here before they blow." Jim Howard was screaming at the top of his lungs now. Although he was a slight, middle-aged man only five-seven, he was built like a wrestler and no one at Leeco dared argue with him.

Sirens echoed across the morning sky, breaking the peaceful serenity of the approaching dawn. Men with fire hoses and fire extinguishers ran chaotically along the dock. Other workers searched the rigs, looking for keys so they could be saved. The Consolidated Freight trailer Gary Martin had been unloading was a mass of smoking ruins. The intensity of the fire had caused the aluminum side panels of the trailer to liquefy, and bubbling streams of aluminum poured to the pavement below the trailer's steel frame.

Men with fire hoses sprayed frantically at the inferno, but the impact of the water caused the blazing boxes to erupt more violently. The eruption sent tiny white-hot fireballs flying in all directions. The fireworks looked like glowing shrapnel from a land mine and the fire wouldn't go out.

All of a sudden, a rig beside the Consolidated trailer exploded from the intense heat and raging fire. The concussion shattered the dock walls. The main support beams holding the roof of the building started to twist and strain under the pressure. The roof sagged and moaned as it collapsed to the dock floor amid showers of intensely burning metal fragments. Debris rained onto the dock, striking everything—including men—there. In seconds, another rig burst into flames as the workers were trying futilely to move all the overroad rigs before fire devoured them.

Frantic dock workers leapt for cover and escaped through any exit large enough to squeeze through. Men were lying on the floor—some screaming, others silent, from their injuries. Gary Martin ran across the blazing dock for an open port. He was leaping for the exit when a flying fireball impacted his lower back and sent him reeling off the dock onto the pavement below. The pain from the blow of the scorching metal slammed him into unconsciousness.

Jim Howard emptied the last of the dry-chemical fire extinguishers at the fire. He took one final look at the inferno and shouted, "Everybody get out of here before she goes totally to hell. Leave the hoses full-cock and haul ass."

The men didn't have to be told twice. They all scrambled for any safety they could find. All of the injured were pulled to the dock edge and lowered to the pavement away from the blaze. The workers waited anxiously across the Leeco terminal lot until the first firefighters arrived and immediately started pumping water onto the roof and the dock. Another fire truck screeched to a stop and more firefighters moved rapidly to extinguish the flames. The more water they pumped onto the original source of the fire, the hotter it became. The building housing the dock was fully aflame. The first responders issued a second and then a third alarm. Soon, the Leeco lot was swarming with firefighters struggling to save anything they could of the building.

In the first minutes they attacked the blaze, the rage of the flames gnawed unrestrainedly at the building structure and consumed every visible carton of freight on the dock. The loss would be high, but at least no one was dead—not yet anyway. Several of the dock workers were suffering from extensive smoke inhalation and burns, but they were all still alive. Paramedics worked quickly and efficiently on the injured. Gary Martin lay prone on a stretcher, awaiting transportation to Dallas General Hospital.

"How you feeling, sport?" Jim Howard asked.

"Like a hot knife gored me," Martin answered.

"You did good. What the hell happened anyway?" Howard asked.

"You got me," Martin said. "I was moving those boxes out of the trailer when the top box burned my hand. It got loose and it fell off the dolly. The next thing I knew, fire was everywhere."

"Strange," Howard said. "Could you tell what was in the cartons?"

"It said something about electronics on the side markings. If they were some electronic gadgets, they sure as shit don't need to be shipped by common carrier."

"Yeah, you're right about that. I think they're ready to move you. I'll be down to see you at the hospital as soon as this clears up a little here."

"Thanks, boss, but I'll be all right."

"See you," Jim Howard said as the paramedics loaded Gary Martin into the ambulance. Then he looked back at the Leeco docks across the parking lot—at his livelihood and the livelihood of all the others scattered around him in disarray. The fire still raged and the sky was filled with towering funnels of black smoke. And the black cloud didn't go away.

The impact of Mike Garland's body knocked the gang leader from his Harley. Both men crashed to the blacktop, the Harley fell over and continued to run in a small circle as the rear wheel kept turning. The other bikers stopped, gathered around the two men, and started chanting. "Kill the mother, B.D. Cut him! Kill him! Cut him! Kill him! Cut him! Kill him . . ."

Both men were up on their feet now, and Garland landed a solid right into the man's bearded jaw. The man named B.D. jerked back from the blow. Then, he brought his right foot up and it slammed into Mike Garland's chest, knocking all breath from him. Garland fell to his knees, gasping. Another foot came up, this one forming a sweeping arch, like a punter with a football, and it flew toward Garland's face. Garland stopped the kick, blocking it with his left arm. He caught his breath and he was up again; his right leg flew through the air with a swivel kick and landed with punishing energy against the biker's head. The man tumbled sideways, blood trickling from a slash left by Garland's boot heel. Mike Garland recaptured his balance from the momentum of his kick. He spun outward, toward the fallen biker, but the man was already up and moving. A shiny fighting knife magically appeared in his right hand. Mike Garland rolled away, dodged a sweeping slash of the blade, and allowed it to cut only air. The knife-wielding man was jabbing, slashing, cutting air as Garland ducked and dodged the lethal onslaught. The biker lunged, thrusting his weight behind the knife in his hand. Garland sidestepped, grabbed the man's wrist, and flipped him, using the momentum of the biker's own movement to complete the throw. B.D. hit the blacktop flat on his back. Garland leapt for his throat, targeting the man's esophagus. B.D. moved, causing Garland's thrust to harmlessly hit the pavement. B.D. swung his legs out and kicked Garland's legs out from under him. Mike Garland fell backward and his head slammed onto the blacktop. The last thing he consciously remembered was darkness descending over everything around him.

CHAPTER TWO

The ringing telephone startled Marc Lee. The Delta Warrior was awake and moving in the bed before the first ring finished. He moved his arm away from Jill Lanier's warm, bare chest and reached for the phone as she snuggled closer to him.

"Lee," he said as he placed the receiver to his ear.

"Marc Lee?" the man calling asked.

"That's right."

"You have a driver named Garland. Maybe I should say *had* a driver named Garland. I have him now. I also have your truck. You should always be sure you finish your work, Marc Lee."

"Who is this?"

"In time you will know. Like, for right now, let's just say I'll be the last face you'll ever see."

"What do you want?" Marc asked as he sat upright in the bed. The bedcover fell from his body, exposing his hairy, muscular chest.

Jill was now fully awake, her captivating bright blue eyes open wide. She tugged at the sheet to cover her naked body. The telephone had startled her too. For a moment, when she looked at Marc beside her in the bed, she felt a flash of guilt like the ones she had felt when they had been in high school together years before. But then she realized they were adults now and responsible to no one but themselves for their actions. The guilt passed and she stared at Marc. She ran her fingers through her twisted blonde hair and tried to straighten it as she listened to Marc's side of the conversation.

"I want you, Marc Lee," the man on the telephone said.

"Okay, so you want me. Why?"

"You killed my snowman and screwed up my business."

"I see—Segalini. Sorry you weren't there, you might have enjoyed the party. Who are you?"

"Not yet, Marc Lee. For now, just understand that I'm your killer. I'm going to kill you with my hands or my knife or maybe even with my gun . . . but I will kill you. You dig?"

"Yeah, I dig. Take your best shot, whoever you are. I'll give you a little advice. Before you try, you need to do some soul-searching because there's something you need to know."

"Like what, Marc Lee?"

"You need to know if your mama raised a fool."

"Another funnyman," the man said, and he laughed. "Why do I always get the funnymen? Mike Garland was a funnyman too, but he's not laughing anymore."

"If you've harmed Mike Garland, I'll find you—whoever you are. I don't think you'll like it when I do."

"Now you're talking my game, Marc Lee. You see, I'm a better man than you are and I was trained by the same people you were. Too bad in Vietnam they didn't understand my way was the right way."

"Your way?"

"Yeah, my way—kill all the bastards and let their maker sort 'em out."

"I think you have problems."

"On that you're right, Marc Lee. I do have problems—Marc Lee and Carl Browne. You see, Leeco is going down into ashes just like Mr. Segalini's house. You messed with my lines, man. Nobody messes with my lines, you dig?"

"You're sick, whoever you are."

"Yeah—I'm sick, but you're dead. Your army made me sick and then you screwed up my lines, man. Now, I'm going to watch you tumble and finish what Bruno Segalini started."

"Bruno Segalini?"

"Hey, man, I don't stutter. That's what I said."

"He's alive?"

"I told you, man, finish what you start," the caller said.

Marc didn't say anything for a long moment. Jill was motionless beside him and her body was warm against his.

Marc ignored the sensual pleasure of her skin against his. His body and mind were at their top survival level. He had to know who this man was.

"Who are you?"

The man on the telephone was laughing hysterically. Suddenly, he stopped. "That worries you, doesn't it? Well, I'm call B.D.—that means Bad Dude. I'll be the last face you ever see, man," B.D. said, and the telephone line went dead.

DON'T MISS
THESE CURRENT
Bantam Bestsellers

Special Offer
Buy a Bantam Book
for only 50¢.

Now you can have Bantam's catalog filled with hundreds of titles plus take advantage of our unique and exciting bonus book offer. A special offer which gives you the opportunity to purchase a Bantam book for only 50¢. Here's how!

By ordering any five books at the regular price per order, you can also choose any other single book listed (up to a $5.95 value) for just 50¢. Some restrictions do apply, but for further details why not send for Bantam's catalog of titles today!

Just send us your name and address and we will send you a catalog!

RELAX!
SIT DOWN
and Catch Up On Your Reading!

☐ 26264 **NATHANIEL** by John Saul $4.50
☐ 27148 **LINES AND SHADOWS** $4.95
        by Joseph Wambaugh
☐ 27386 **THE DELTA STAR** $4.95
        by Joseph Wambaugh
☐ 27259 **GLITTER DOME** $4.95
        by Joseph Wambaugh
☐ 26757 **THE LITTLE DRUMMER GIRL** $4.95
        by John Le Carré
☐ 26705 **SUSPECTS** by William J. Cavnitz $4.95
☐ 26657 **THE UNWANTED** by John Saul $4.50
☐ 26658 **A GRAND PASSION** by Mary Mackey $4.50
☐ 26499 **LAST OF THE BREED** by $4.50
        Louis L'Amour
☐ 27430 **THE SECRETS OF HARRY BRIGHT** by $4.95
        Joseph Wambaugh

Masterful Intrigue
by the Intriguing Master

☐ **THE BOURNE IDENTITY** 45053/$14.95

He is a man with an unknown past and an uncertain future. A man dragged from the sea riddled with bullets, his face altered by plastic surgery—a man bearing the dubious identity of Jason Bourne.

Now the story of Jason Bourne comes to life in this exciting double cassette adaptation with a stirring reading by Darren McGavin.   (125 minutes)

☐ **THE MATARESE CIRCLE** 45088/$14.95

They are sworn mortal enemies, one Russian, one American. To save the world they must swallow their hate and work together to break the MATARESE CIRCLE.

Martin Balsam dramatizes this double cassette abridgement of Ludlum's national bestseller.   (180 minutes)

☐ **LUDLUM ON LUDLUM** 45027/$7.95

Ludlum's insights into the world of political intrigue suggest that he has connections to the world of espionage he writes about. How has he come to know the secrets of the CIA and the KGB? Where and why did he learn to write spy thrillers that have shocked and delighted millions? In this tape Robert Ludlum reveals all.   (60 minutes)

Look for them at your bookstore or use this page to order.